ADIRONDACK AUGUST

A Novel

By

KAY BENEDICT SGARLATA

Adirondack August

ISBN-10: 0615817610
ISBN-13: 9780615817613
Library of Congress Control Number: 2013909364
Kay Benedict Sgarlata Syracuse, NY

ACKNOWLEDGMENTS

After writing two memoirs, I was emboldened to try my hand at completing a novel. Only with the support of family and friends, and a great writing coach in David Hazard, was this possible.

I have numerous people to thank—first and foremost my husband Tony, who always has been there for me. I also am grateful to my siblings, Dorothy, Donald, Barbara, and Carol, who, having traveled to our family camp in the Adirondack Mountains, supported my effort to write a fictional work set in the area we all have known since birth.

I'd also like to thank my test readers and editors, Katy Benson, June Rose, Bill Bell, Kathy Morris, and Reggie Chambers. I offer a special thank-you to Cynthia Haythe for her writing skills and unique ability to share constructive criticism with me along the way. Thanks also go to my dear friend Sandi Slowik Galler, the best of editors, who was ever encouraging. She continued to challenge me, for which I extend my heartfelt appreciation. And last but not least, thank you to the members of my book club, whose kind words have served to empower me since I began my writing career.

This book, my first novel, takes place in the central Adirondack Mountains. Although the contents and characters are fictitious, I have attempted to stay true to the geography of New York State.

My hope is that readers can grow in an appreciation of the vast Adirondack Park, feel its chilly mornings, and smell the essence of balsam and pine.

I dedicate *Adirondack August* to my husband Tony who, for the past thirty years, has paddled the lakes and hiked the trails of the Adirondacks with me.

PROLOGUE

"Hey, Sarge," yelled David. "Are you just about ready?"

"Give me a few more minutes," Chris responded. She wanted to be sure everything was in order, all details double-checked.

The song of locusts filled the Victorian homestead as Christine Wright, who always needed to be on top of everything, moved through each room like a woman on a mission. The thermometer affixed to the outside of the kitchen window revealed that it was already in the low eighties on this mid-August Saturday in Cooperstown, New York. Her husband was almost finished packing the car, and in a few minutes, he'd be pressing her to get on the road.

Chris, with her well-ordered mental checklist, went about the routine she had followed dozens of times in preparation for a week's vacation at the family's camp. In this spacious house where she had grown up and had returned with her own family after her mother's passing in 1988, she had a well-developed schedule that worked for her. While David hauled luggage and food to the car, she dashed up the green-carpeted staircase to make sure that all of the windows were down and that the faucets in the two bathrooms weren't dripping. On her descent to the foyer, she mentally screened her to-do list.

As she went from room to room, she realized her ability to concentrate on present duties was nonexistent.. Unexplained feelings of unsettledness overwhelmed her this morning. As she watched David carry their bags and provisions to the car, a flood of memories overtook her. She could see her mother Mary layering blankets and pillows on the backseat of their sedan—which were necessary for their stay at camp—and providing comfort to Chris and her siblings for the ride ahead. She recalled that when the smell and crunch of falling leaves and crispness had filled the air, deer hunting season became the magnet that pulled her dad to the North Woods. In the early 1950s, her spry and active grandparents packed up their own Buick, anticipation filling them—and a few of Dad's friends—as they departed Cooperstown, located in southeastern New York State, to make the 105-mile trek. The men had every assurance that they'd bag a couple of deer during the trip.

The unsettled feelings didn't make sense. These people and camp were Chris's solid foundation, everything her life had been built upon. She saw the images in full color, as if they'd just occurred.

For some reason she didn't understand, the past was strangely present, as if her life were as circular as this annual trek from this home, in this small town, to what she knew to be her real home, her family's cabin tucked safely in the mountains.

For a moment she wondered, *Why does the past seem so important right now?*

After Chris had checked all the rooms, she reentered the foyer. She closed the large wooden front door and turned the brass key in the deadbolt lock. Key in hand, she turned and glanced at the multitude of framed photographs that lined the mint-green walls; as with most things this morning, an unexplained interest drew her in.

In fact this mood had been coming and going for several days. She couldn't put her finger on it but wondered whether it was the time of the year—August, when summer had turned the corner.

She was aware of the slight touches of autumn coolness in the morning and evening air. She had been reflecting on yet another season's passing.

She paused, thinking that perhaps it was a result of age and having lost so many who were dear to her. As she gazed upon the generations of Wrights whose pictures animated the wall, their images beckoned her. Slowly she lifted a silver-framed picture taken on her mother and father's twenty-fifth wedding anniversary.

Her index finger touched her father's face, as if to feel his strength and encouragement once more. It was not the norm in her childhood to think of her father clean-shaven and in a suit, white shirt and tie, which the photograph revealed. When she saw him in her minds-eye he was in bib overalls, scruffy in appearance and at the lumber mill. She noted, however, each Sunday he had dressed up to go to church, the one day of the week that he did rest and relax with his family. Her Dad always had a smile on his face and the camera had certainly captured it here.

She ran her finger over her mother's face as she recalled her stately beauty, remembering and admiring the two piece aqua-blue outfit her mother had purchased for the anniversary celebration When dressed in high heels, her Mom stood two inches taller than her Dad. She was thin but well-proportioned and walked with an elegant air about her. She had served as Chris' role model – well-spoken, professional and organized. Chris always felt she had been especially blessed when it came to her parents; they had been loving, kind, and supportive. How many times had they loaded their children into the family car for the trip she and David were about to make? Of all the places she had lived over her sixty-eight years, Lake Wrights—the name her dad christened his lakefront cottage—had been that one constant; it was always there, never changing, stable. It was her heart's true home, a refuge created by her father, whom she had adored.

Until David had entered Chris's life, she had looked upon her parents as her rocks, especially her father. Is that why he seemed so close now? Was she thinking of everything he had given her?

It would take her father three tries to produce a son. In the meantime Chris, as the firstborn, had served as her father's helper, his sidekick. For a dozen years, she had served in that role until the baby of the family, Hal, Jr., turned eight. It wasn't as if Harold Wright had needed help. Although he stood only five seven and tipped the scales as a middleweight, he was built like a bull and by skill and boundless energy had been able to outwork most men. His face and hands were ruddy, but Chris always looked at him as a kind of Santa Claus—kind, gentle, and generous to a fault.

In 1950 her dad had purchased a heavily wooded lakefront property on Seventh Lake, just beyond the tiny hamlet of Inlet, on the western side of the huge Adirondack Park. A wild landscape of mountains and lakes cradled the Wright cabin. Chris never ceased to be amazed by her father's imagination, how he had created a blueprint and started construction with the help of his two brothers and a few male friends. It was during that year of building that Chris began her seasonal treks to Seventh Lake. As an eight-year-old, she lent an occasional hand after begging her father to take her along.

From the earliest time she could remember, Chris entered a world of her own each time she traveled north from Cooperstown to the Adirondack Mountains. Each spring, as the world reawakened around her, and as the earth warmed along with its lakes and streams, her whole being desired to be in her imagined Eden—the special place she had grown to love, the one filled with the essence of balsam and pine, sweet odors of the earth, and a lake whose refreshing water soothed every bit of her stress and anxiety.

It had been decades since she had thought as a child did, and yet she still possessed that same longing to return to the North Woods, the term her dad always used when referring to the Adirondacks. Why were memories of her dad so present in her this morning?

David would be coming in at any moment to gently steer her toward the car, his patience, if not his kindness, playing out. Now, as she glanced up and looked intently at another picture of her father, taken when he was in his midthirties, she saw vividly the tent she had shared with him when the family camp was under construction and she was so happy to be along on a couple of work-party weekends.

The camp wasn't just the family's gathering place. Chris thought of this camp in the North Woods as her own special place.

Though her dad's original plan for the camp had been a hunting and fishing lodge, he discovered it was also the perfect family vacation place. Chris always had thought of the month of August as the alpha and the omega in her relationship with Lake Wrights because it was the beginning of a new school year after a time of refreshment, relaxation, and renewal, as well as the end of another camp season. Her emotions ran high as she recalled how many times in late August her mother would say, "Now, Chris, stop crying. You know you'll be back in November." But being there in November wasn't the same for Chris, who loved the freedom to hike and swim and run about with as little clothing on as her mother would allow.

With the picture frame still clutched in her hands, she glanced back at the wall, where professionally taken photographs hung of her grandparents. As she gazed at the photos, she thought of her valued lineage. Directly after high school, her father, Harold, had followed his own father's path into the lumber business, never giving thought to a college education. Chris always had been impressed with his knowledge, not only of the world of lumber but also the world in general. She played at the profession on Saturday mornings when she'd check out the new piles of lumber that had arrived during the week, hang out with the men from town who were there to make purchases, and wander through the barns and sheds that comprised the complex. When she found herself alone in a back corner, she had a ball pretending that she was the boss, and she'd instruct an imaginary workman that he needed to remove eighteen four-by-sixes that Mr. Jones would be picking up later in the day. That was important, she thought—to be in charge.

A feeling of being in control also was important to her. She had learned this by observing her father as he engaged his clients. It was crucial to know everything you had in stock, what could be ordered, and how long it would take for delivery—in sum, how to keep everything under your thumb.

Chris jolted back to reality when she heard the bang of the back screen door. "How much longer, Chris?" David asked her. Before she could respond, he walked into the foyer. Noting the picture frame in her hand, he sensed that his wife of thirty-four years was deep in thought. He bent his well-built six-foot frame and kissed Chris on the top of the head. Placing his hands gently on her shoulders, he offered, "Let me run down to Eric's, fill up the tank, and pick you up on my way back."

She glanced up into David's brown eyes, which elicited a smile from her. "Sounds good. I'll bring along the thermos of coffee."

Knowing she now had a few more minutes, she sat down on the parson's bench and relaxed.

She thought that just as camp held some of her happiest memories, so did this family home, but they also held some of her most bitter memories. She had assigned those life experiences to a hidden room in the recesses of her mind, where she rarely, if ever, allowed herself to go. This morning was no different.

What she held onto was an invisible link that anchored her in family, tradition, a work ethic, and faith. Individually her mother and father had spent hours, as they both neared their end days, sharing some of the most intimate memories of their lives, tender moments that caused Chris to frequently break down and cry.

Her father had outlived her mom by almost thirteen years and had welcomed Chris and her family back to this family home after her mom's passing. Chris thought back on those years as being the greatest gift she'd ever received. Those years with dad were so special—precious time when her father had shared so many of his life stories with her.

Her review of the Wright family photo gallery now complete, she rose, re-hung the picture frame, and headed toward the kitchen. The grandfather clock at the back of the entryway struck nine, and Chris stood there as the antique clock chimed each hour, her eyes focusing on the old marble-topped table that sat alongside it. A family phone, whatever the design, had occupied its place there as long as she could remember, and Chris recalled the countless calls she had received—joy-filled, memorable, and heartbreaking. Momentarily her thoughts drifted to some painful phone calls.

Stop, Chris. Don't even go there, she thought. Yes, there were darker moments from the past as well, but she didn't want to linger on those. She only wanted to remember the brightness of what she'd lived.

As she entered the kitchen, she filled the thermos for her and David to drink on the way and had enough coffee left in the pot to fill half her cup.

A few minutes later, the sound of the car's horn rousted Chris from her thoughts. She rinsed out her empty ceramic cup emblazoned with NATIONAL BASEBALL HALL OF FAME on it, placed it in the dishwasher, and grabbed the thermos and the morning paper. She made her way out the kitchen door using the brass key and locked up the house. David pulled the Chrysler 300 closer to the side door as Chris headed to the driver's side. It was time to shake off the unsettled mood that had tried to take her over—but who knew why it had appeared?

Let the past be the past, she thought. *Life is about living in the now. Take the good from the past and leave the dark and unpleasant behind.*

As David lowered the window, Chris asked, "How about if I drive? That way you can read the paper."

David climbed out from behind the steering wheel, then bent down and planted a quick kiss on Chris's lips. "That works for me."

Chapter 1

A red Ford truck pulling a trailer with twin Sea-Doos crept alongside Chris and David's car in the left-hand lane. Chris snapped out of her daydream and glanced at her speedometer, which read fifty-five. She blinked her eyes as she wondered how many miles she had covered, oblivious to any of her scenic surroundings. Had other vehicles passed them? She couldn't be sure. She had seen the familiar signs and structures she'd become familiar with over the years of traveling this route. They now served as a visual assurance that she'd only been in her reverie for a few minutes.

The heat from the August sun permeated the sunroof; even the air conditioner couldn't eliminate the moisture from her skin. Just about sixty years had passed since that first trip, when her family had traveled north out of Cooperstown, through the lush, green Mohawk River Valley.

In the early years, the ride from home to camp seemed to take forever as they journeyed past farms and fields. Today she noted that the topography and landscape were compellingly familiar. Chris refocused and, as she looked about, could not have imagined a more ideal setting for her daydreaming as she drove north on a picture-perfect day.

David was buried in the morning paper; neither of them had found the need to listen to NPR. She made the slight right turn onto Route 28, where they quickly departed an environment of farmland, meadows, and streams and entered a pathway of rivers and towering pines that brought a rapid rise in elevation. Chris remembered her mother's words from many Novembers past as they had crossed over the Black River in Forestport, thirty minutes north of Utica—"Now say a prayer that we make it up the hill."

Today's trip over the "new and improved" roadway was no challenge, unlike the difficulties encountered in the past, when Route 28 had meandered through the hamlet, winding its way up a steep hill to the summit, where car and tire performance was always questionable.

Even though Chris had tried to shake the past, it was impossible to escape the memories along this road. It was where her father had shared fascinating stories with his children of his arrival in the Adirondacks as a young boy. Her ears perked up as he shared not only his recollections but also his knowledge of the North Woods. The three-hour trip passed more quickly as her dad recalled his fishing and hunting excursions with his father and uncles. It became apparent to Chris that from an early age her father had grown to love and value these Adirondack Mountains. He shared encounters he'd had with the guides and the locals. What had he said? "We're now traveling through the southwestern part of the largest park in the United States. The Adirondacks have some of the newest mountains in North America and are made up of some of the continent's oldest rocks."

She remembered how her father often had effortlessly rattled off numbers as well. "You know, kids," he'd say, "there are close to three thousand lakes and ponds here in the park." Chris always would ask herself, *How does he know that?*

Her dad loved to talk about his boyhood days—hunting in the late fall with his father and how he had come to appreciate the flora and fauna of the mountains. Although her father had been a "go to church every Sunday" Catholic, Chris hadn't known him to be religious. However, when he spoke of the forty-two peaks that were more than four thousand feet in elevation, and of the hundreds of acres of old-growth forest, and of God's great creation here in New York State, she sensed a spiritual connection with his passionate words that she hadn't heard before.

Chris decided to open the sunroof. In the old days, in the summertime, when the windows were all rolled down, this portion of the trip was the first time they'd get a good whiff of the scent of the pines.

Oh, my, she thought. *What we all lose today with air-conditioned cars and windows closed up tighter than a drum, keeping out the natural scents and sounds.*

She recalled saying, "Oh, Daddy, doesn't this smell good? It's like the great smells when the logs at the mill are sawed."

Her father would agree and talk about the timber he ordered regularly that was cut here and delivered to Cooperstown for him to process and sell. What followed was Hal Wright sharing the history of his father having founded the Wright Lumber Mill thirty years prior. Chris and her siblings had heard the story many times, but they never tired of his retelling it. Everyone seemed to know he took great pride in the business that provided a very good income for his family and for many others in the town.

Chris thought that perhaps one of the reasons her dad loved the Adirondacks so much was because of his love of wood. As a child even she had come to recognize trees by their bark and leaves and had learned to distinguish the different smells of various pieces and cuts of lumber.

Keep your mind on your driving, she thought. Shortly she crossed over the Blue Line, the imaginary line around the six-million-acre Adirondack Park, though an actual demarcation on many maps.

Chris murmured to herself, "Ah, the beauty of the Adirondacks! We're here again to enjoy your crystal-clear lakes, babbling brooks, and dark, dense forests."

Right on schedule, the sign that read, ENTERING THE ADIRONDACK PARK appeared, and she knew that in another ten minutes they'd approach the McKeever Bridge, which passed over Moose River.

When Chris had grown into her twenties, she frequently drove this route alone and remembered how symbolic the bridge had become to her; it was the passage between home and camp, the point of leaving behind and going to.

Out of the corner of her eye, she caught David's glance. He didn't interrupt what he sensed was another of his wife's "out of body experiences." David was well aware of how completely she could become absorbed in a thought or memory, lose all track of time and place, and simply enjoy her daydream. He quickly returned to reading the opinion page.

David was correct. Chris was enjoying the splendor of the moment, catching glimpses of her past, as if an instant replay of earlier times were being rebroadcast in living color. She was lost in things inside herself. The flood of memories that had begun early this morning continued, not only the good and enjoyable but also the dark ones—those that were heartbreaking, painful, and hidden to this day.

Chris wondered whether it was late in adolescence when she had read and memorized the lines from Tennyson's poem "Ulysses." She silently recited them now, as she often did. *I am a part of all I have met: yet each experience is an arch where thru gleams that untravel'd world.*

They were the words that gave her comfort, words that allowed her to embrace every aspect of her life: the good, the bad, the moments of great joy, and those she struggled with daily.

Raised a Catholic, Chris always had practiced her faith and had been married in the church—twice. Thank God (or was it the Pope?) for annulments. After discovering the essence of her faith in her midthirties, she continued to grow in a deeper and more satisfying relationship with the God she had known since childhood. Her daily meditation gave her life richness; she felt at peace. Or at least that's what she told herself. Silently and alone she harbored the unresolved issues of her life. To all who knew her she was "Miss Confident"; she had it all together. That's how Chris wanted it. That's the way she lived her life. Her credo was "Live in the moment and don't look back."

Chris reflected on living in the moment and instantaneously jumped back to reality as the car passed over Moose River. She took a quick look down in both directions, checking the level of the shallow river and watching the sun play upon the water from her vantage point two hundred feet above. Frequently in late spring, filled with melted snow, it would be running high and raging. Today it was low and flowed gently over countless rocks, creating a picturesque and tranquil scene. Far to her right, she spotted tree-covered mountains.

Another ten minutes, and we'll be approaching Old Forge, Chris thought. She realized that over the years she had played time games all the way to camp. It had been a pleasant distraction when she had traveled alone—ten minutes from one hamlet to the next along the way. She knew it was silly, but for her it moved the time along, and every ten minutes she could check off meant she was that much closer to her beloved camp.

The late-morning sun prompted Chris to grab the sunglasses she had tossed on the dash earlier. She slowed the car to a crawl through Old Forge, situated at the head of the Fulton Chain of Lakes. The busy little resort community was at the height of tourist season, and today was typical of that time of year, as she paused several times to allow eager and preoccupied vacationers to dash across the main street from one souvenir shop to another.

Her twenty-minute drive continued along the ascending numbered lakes that stretched to Fourth Lake near Inlet. Throughout the trip Chris had noticed David's smiling glances, and she had responded silently by extending her hand to caress the top of his.

She loved being embraced by David but was frequently overcome simply by his unspoken look or touch. Chris thought, *How blessed this thirty-four year marriage to David has been.*

October 16, 1976 was the Saturday when she and David Herring had wed. Their plan to marry had been a bit unorthodox, but the intervening years had stood as a testament to the desire each possessed to have it succeed.

She had met David soon after beginning her newspaper career at the *Utica Herald and Courier.* He already had been on staff for a year, reporting local news, before she had signed on to cover the political scene. On her drive home to Clinton, New York, each night, she often reflected on the day, her conversations with David, and his willingness to answer her never-ending questions. Oh, how she valued and appreciated his work ethic, his thoughtfulness, his ability to uncover the smallest detail in investigating a news story. David was her model of a true professional—ethical, moral, truthful, and compassionate.

They had adjoining cubicles and grew fond of each other as they shared some of the difficulties each was experiencing in their young marriages. Over the next five years, David and his wife, Jean had two children, Gregory and DeEtte. Chris celebrated with them as each baby arrived and showered them with gifts. Only once over the years had David asked Chris whether she planned to have children, and her response had been, "One of these days."

She did want children, and in the early years of her marriage, it wasn't for lack of trying. When she and Mike separated nine years into their marriage, David listened and offered support. At the same time, Chris was there for David and his children as he dealt with Jean's breast cancer, which didn't have a favorable prognosis. Early the next year, David was a widower, and Chris was about to file for divorce.

In early 1976 they began to date. For both, it was awkward at first. Having been such good friends and confidants for so long, the transition to a romantic relationship took some time. But they found themselves comfortable in each others presence and their ability to share conversations openly and honestly, created a strong bond. That summer, when Chris's annulment was finalized, they first spoke of marriage.

That year Chris invited a very happy and receptive David, Gregory, and DeEtte to the family camp for Labor Day weekend. She committed herself to him and shared their marriage plans to the delight of David's children and her mom and dad. In the following days and weeks, their friends, coworkers, and extended family looked forward to the big day.

Chris's daydreaming was interrupted when David said, "Sometimes I don't really appreciate how much you're into this place."

For the last half-hour, he'd been listening to the CD Chris had been playing, *A Loon Symphony*, which incorporated two of the things she liked best—the strains of the classics and the sounds of the Adirondack wilderness, especially the songs of the loon.

"You're right," Chris said. "Even if I live to be a hundred, there isn't enough time to take it all in."

In just five minutes, they'd be at camp. Fourth Lake was glittering off to the right in the noonday sunshine as she drove toward the tiny hamlet of Inlet, where campers and summer tourists could procure supplies and groceries, grab a cold beer, purchase a good book or an ice cream cone, and if so inclined, recreate in the large park nestled in the heart of the village.

Chris had known this village since those early years. She thought, *Wasn't it Mrs. Greeley at the post office who always said, 'Hello, little girl' every time I went along with Dad as he mailed something back to the mill?*

She recalled frolicking up and down the old wooden floors of the tiny grocery store as her mother found bread and milk on the shelves. Chris always shrieked with delight when her dad announced after supper that they were going to drive the mile-and-a-half back to Inlet for frozen custard. Oh, those special summertime memories.

This was one more August when Chris could reflect, as she thought not only of those innocent days of youth but also of all the years that her own children had been enriched by their experiences at camp. August always seemed to provide those long, hot memorable days that resonated with her from long ago. And she often quoted from the 1960s Nat King Cole hit—"Those hazy, lazy, crazy days of summer… Those days of soda and pretzels and beer…"—and sometimes even sang the refrain aloud.

Even now the thought of it prompted her to hum a few bars as she slowed down along the narrow two-lane road through the village. They'd be at camp momentarily.

Chris always enjoyed the warm feeling of anticipation she experienced when she knew their youngest son, Ron, would be there to greet them. Ron had grown to love the camp and regularly took advantage of the retreat when he could escape his priestly duties for a few days. This coming week was no exception.

Here she was, once again this morning, thinking of her family members. How could she not embrace warm thoughts of Greg and DeEtte, the stepchildren whom she considered her own? Chris relished the days in August when her growing family had spent precious time at the camp. Her three kids had kept her occupied with the work of motherhood—a time that was much too busy to allow her the opportunity to concentrate on her own worries or concerns. But her children had grown up, and now she did have time for serious reflection. Why couldn't this week at camp be like it had been so many years earlier, with kids and laughter filling Lake Wrights?

Although Greg and DeEtte both had loved the time they'd spent at the family camp, after his graduation from Syracuse University, Greg had a mind of his own, and Chris always laughed to herself when she thought, *Where did he get that from?* He saw himself in uniform, serving his country, and met with a marine recruiter within days of his return home from college.

Long discussions took place at the kitchen table, especially between Greg and David. Although Chris supported Greg's decision, she often remembered that she wasn't his biological mother and probably should leave the deeper, more sensitive issues to the two of them.

When Greg's body was returned for burial in April 1991, Chris was as much at a loss for words as David. Soon after his enlistment and basic training, he had been sent to Bangladesh to assist with humanitarian efforts after the devastating tropical cyclone had killed 138,000 and left ten million homeless.

Just months earlier Chris had begun to pray that he wouldn't be sent to the Persian Gulf for Operation Desert Storm and felt very relieved when he wasn't. The news that the helicopter in which he was being transported had gone down accidentally with all aboard killed was incomprehensible.

Greg was buried with full military honors in the plot next to his mother's. Chris and David made a pilgrimage there each Sunday that first year.

In the months and years that followed, Chris did her best at keeping alive the good times, the memories that Greg had helped to create. Taking frequent trips to the camp, scanning through photo albums, and supporting DeEtte as she finished her degree at Chris's alma mater, the State University of New York at Oneonta, all seemed to help her.

David on the other hand, was overwhelmed with grief. Chris sensed he was making every effort to portray himself as a grieving father who could control his emotions. He continued his daily work routine. He performed his household chores without skipping a beat. Whenever he was alone, however, he cried. More than once, Chris had seen him slumped over the lawn mower, sobbing. Her heart ached when she heard his crying through the bathroom door. It wasn't uncommon, after running errands, for him to sit in the car until he regained his composure.

David took solace in prayer and found strength from good friends who were good listeners and allowed him to talk about his son whenever he chose, whether on the golf course or over a beer.

A year-and-a-half after Greg's passing, Chris noticed that David had begun to speak about his son in conversations, without breaking down. He brought up his name frequently by saying, "Do you remember when Greg…"

Time had been a wonderful healer.

A year after her graduation, DeEtte had moved to Atlanta to begin her journalism career, landing a post at CNN, immersing herself in work, and discovering the love of her life. Chris always thought of her stepdaughter as being beautiful and talented and possessing many of her late mother's traits. She hadn't been a problem to raise, but like her brother Greg, she was fiercely independent.

It was rare that DeEtte and her family departed Atlanta to vacation in New York State. But when they did, the camp was most often their destination, which allowed Chris and David the opportunity to spoil their two grandkids and provided DeEtte the chance to recapture her best camp memories through shared stories in front of the fireplace.

So the roots of the family here at the camp were very deep—as deep as the roots of the Jack pines, as deep as the mountain streams and river gorges. Here at camp they had laughed and cried, loved and grieved losses. Here was where Chris had found herself woven into her family, her life. Just like Grandma Wright's patchwork quilt that lay at the foot of the brass bed in the camp loft, the family's history, Chris knew, was imperfect, sometimes mismatched but from a distance appearing absolutely perfect. She often thought that as long as no one looked too closely, everything seemed to be in order.

The left-hand turn into the camp driveway required a wait, as there was a stream of oncoming traffic—SUVs carrying canoes and kayaks, cars and trucks pulling motor craft and pontoon boats, the Adirondack toys of summer. Small outboard motorboats weren't uncommon fifty years ago, but today's inboard and personal watercraft increasingly competed with the quieter, gentler canoes and kayaks. Perhaps something *had* changed over the years—the noise level on the roads and waterways.

CHAPTER 2

The day was bright as the noon sun filtered through the hardwoods and towering white pines that encroached upon the driveway, greeting Chris as usual. The clock on the dash confirmed for her that once again the drive had taken two hours and ten minutes, door to door.

In midsummer the lofty trees served as a canopy in various shades of green. She had no way of knowing just how many times she had ridden or driven down this dirt-and-gravel driveway to Lake Wrights. Each time she felt an excitement, the feeling of being a kid again. She proceeded slowly, so as not to kick up stones against the silver Chrysler, and eased the car into the well-worn parking area at the rear of the camp, where Ron already had parked his black Jeep Liberty.

Before she could open the car door, he appeared on the back porch, his thin five-foot-eleven frame decked out in a pair of tan Bermuda shorts and a yellow golf shirt. More often than not, she saw her son sans Roman collar, and yet it always surprised her. He was barefoot, and for the first time, Chris noticed that his hair might be receding, thinning a bit. He was indeed his mother's son, bearing her physical characteristics—blond hair, hazel eyes, and fair skin. Chris considered him handsome and thought, *Doesn't God always take the best-looking ones for himself?*

Ron greeted his mother with his typical bear hug and shouted over the roof of the car, "Hi, Dad," as David emerged from the passenger seat. Chris wished he had made the effort to take the short walk to David's side of the car and give him a hug also, but she knew that wasn't going to happen.

"Give me the keys, Mom, and I'll unload," Ron offered, as Chris retrieved her purse, sunglasses, and water bottle. As he popped open the trunk, he added, "Thanks for packing light."

The small back wooden deck held two plastic chairs and provided a view of nothing, save the cars, an outbuilding used for storage, and the woods. The camp sat fifty feet from the water's edge, and from the back deck, the property remained flat for another fifty feet before the land rose sharply up to Route 28. The original outhouse also stood back there; no longer in use, it was a symbol of the "once upon a time" days at camp. Still they had maintained it over the years, in case of emergency and for nostalgia's sake; its presence served as a catalyst for many an opening conversation for visitors.

On most days at camp, Chris found her way to one of the chairs on the back porch, to sit in the late afternoon, meditating. The space provided quiet, with minimal distractions. She loved the solitude of this place. Depending on the time of the year, she could see in her view a rare lady's slipper in bloom or trilliums, sometimes a Jack-in-the-pulpit, and always breathe in deeply the fragrance of the pines.

She encouraged the local chipmunks by placing a few peanuts on the back steps to entice them to come closer. They always did, filling their jowls with the nuts then scampering off to a nest to deposit them and quickly returning for more. Chris always knew what she had started and ceased after they had gathered around a dozen peanuts. She'd refocus on what her real purpose was in coming to this place.

With the thermos tucked under his arm, David held open the screen door, which was well worn from the countless trips in and out with luggage and provisions over the years. After wiping his feet on the welcome mat, Ron carried the few bags and boxes into the hallway. Chris already had made her way quickly through the long hallway that led to the living room, simultaneously catching the aromas of pine and coffee.

"Oh, it's good to be back," she said under her breath.

Ron obviously had been at camp long enough to light the scented candles on the mantle and brew a pot of decaf. The front door and windows were open, helping to air out the interior and allowing for the sounds of motorboats, seaplanes, and the shouts of happy children, perhaps from a neighboring cottage, to create a pleasant camp welcome.

"Mom, where do you want me to put the clean sheets?" Ron asked, holding the canvas bag in his hand.

"Just give them to me," Chris replied. "I'll put them in the chest of drawers."

Taking the bag of clean linens, Chris walked into the bedroom she had called hers since her first husband Mike and she had come to camp after their marriage in 1965. She glanced around the twelve-by-twelve-foot space, a bedroom virtually unchanged in all the years the camp had stood. Her grandparents had first occupied it; it was Grandpa Wright who had encouraged Hal, when building the camp, to use cedar and knotty pine for the walls. And so cedar planking covered the two downstairs bedroom walls, and knotty pine provided the walls for the rest of the main floor. The warmth and endurance of the blond wood appealed to Chris in this mountain retreat.

After she placed the sheets in the bureau drawer, she rested her hand on the warm wood, as if absorbing its strength, steadiness, and endurance. Chris often was surprised when the wood seemed to emit the scent of her mother's cigarette smoke or the hint of her perfume, her dad's sweat or his pipe tobacco, all of which was long held within the grain. She remembered how her father's camp, originally built as a hunting lodge, had been transformed into the family's vacation spot in the warm weather months. Well into the 1970s,

Hal Wright and his brothers and buddies had mounted an effort to manage to get in at least one weekend of hunting in November, staying at the camp and sharing memories of previous years.

A decade later, however, with the men's increased age and seeming lack of interest, the camp ceased to be the magnet that drew them to the hunting outpost.

Now this camp that her dad and his friends had built sixty years ago was her family's warm-weather escape. Chris often remarked to David and her kids that she still felt the presence of her grandparents and parents whenever she spent time here. They had provided her with countless memories of Lake Wrights. Each successive time she arrived, those strong family connections continued to be reinforced, every memory stirred up again. The Wrights of an earlier time were gone, but every experience she'd shared with them had been etched not only in her head but also in her heart. Here, in a cabin shared by generations of her family, Chris felt deeply rooted and stable. Unshakeable.

"Are you sleeping up or down this time?" Chris asked Ron as she emerged from the bedroom and found him still standing in the kitchen. She patted his upper arm as she passed.

"Since no one else will be here this week but us, I figured I'd take the whole upstairs," he responded with a smile, as he handed her a cup of hot coffee.

Chris uttered a quick "Thank you," always so pleased that Ron fixed her coffee perfectly, with just the right amounts of sweetener and milk.

The square kitchen appeared to be bigger than it was, due to her dad's decision to leave open the interior walls above the countertops. It allowed for many folks to engage in kitchen conversations without having to step foot onto its linoleum floor. The knotty-pine room and cupboards were both rustic and highly functional, having undergone some of her dad's remodeling over the years to accommodate a refrigerator that replaced an old oak icebox. He also had brightened the room with the addition of a side window. Now the kitchen sported a microwave, coffeemaker, and toaster oven as well.

Chris put away the groceries then headed to the living room/ dining room that filled the front of the camp. To the left of the stone fireplace that dominated the front wall was the natural cedar staircase that led to the second-floor loft and two additional bedrooms.

As a child Chris had spent many hours in the cozy loft where old iron and brass double beds filled the rooms, bedecked with patchwork quilts passed down from her Mrs. Beasley–looking Grandma Wright. Here, on many rainy summer afternoons, she and her siblings had played games, sat and talked, or lay on their beds to read books they had checked out from the Cooperstown village library, or in Chris's case, one or two that had been secretly removed from the bookcase at home, where her mother placed books she had read.

Did Chris's mother need to know she was reading *Tea and Sympathy* or *On the Beach*? Thirty years later, when rain kept the kids indoors, Greg and DeEtte joined Ron, and at times the silence from the loft was deafening. She wondered what the kids were up there reading, but she didn't worry. She had great faith and trust in her children's reading choices.

"Hey, Mom. I left the local weeklies on the table for you." Ron's voice shattered Chris's brief reverie. "I wiped down the counters too. There were some mouse droppings."

Moments like this always reminded Chris that although she loved this camp, summertime brought out the mice, black flies, and mosquitoes. They were annoyances to be sure but hardly enough to cause frustration.

Ron walked into the living room carrying a piece of his mother's German plum-topped kuchen. Knowing Ron's weakness for this cake, one that his Grandma Wright and regularly made, Chris had baked it the day before and made sure David packed it for the trip. "I stopped to pick up some charcoal at the store on my way through Inlet and picked up the papers," he told her. "I knew you'd want to read the latest issues."

How funny. Chris and Dave subscribed to the weekly central Adirondack papers, which arrived by third-class mail five or six days after publication. Her "nose for news" always prompted her to pick them up locally—hot off the presses—soon after she arrived at camp.

From the time Chris had grown serious about being a journalist during her sophomore year at Oneonta, she had become energized when newsprint lay in front of her and the ink rubbed off on her fingers. All these years later, she hadn't forgotten the field trip to Albany to watch a newspaper being "put to bed." She asked the newsmen every question she could imagine and wanted to know the process from beginning to end. Today, just like every other day when she held a newspaper, she knew every detail that had made the publication possible.

From her vantage point, as she sat at the dining room table, Chris could see clear to the dock. She noticed through the front window that the canoe was already in the water, and David was pulling the kayak from its storage location alongside the camp. This was the routine Hal Wright had followed each time he had come to the camp in summer, and David wanted to be a good steward and follow, as best he could, all the practices his late father-in law had established.

"Oh, my God," Chris said, as she brought her right hand to her chest.

"What is it, Mom?" Ron asked as he walked into the living room.

Trying to calm herself from the shock, Chris reported, "It's the obituary of a man named Fred Taylor. Back in the fifties, he and his family rented the camp up the lake."

"Was he anyone I ever knew?" Ron probed.

"No," Chris stated emphatically.

"What was his name again?

All Chris could think was, *What have I started? If I hadn't gasped, he would have no idea what I was reading.*

She went back to her reading. Not wanting to bring any more attention to the issue than she already had, she calmed herself and simply said, "Frederick Taylor. He lived in Cortland, but apparently in recent times he summered on Raquette Lake, which apparently is the reason they're covering his passing in the paper."

"How old was he?" Ron asked. "If he was renting a place next door in the fifties, he must have been Grandpa's age."

"You're right. Says he was born in nineteen twenty. He was ninety. He obviously lived a long, full life."

"When you're done, let me read it, Mom. Is there a picture?"

"Yes. From what I can remember of him, I'd say he changed over the years. He was much thinner than he was sixty years ago, and his hair was shorter back then. I remember him having a brush cut." Chris was guarding her words. "Let me get through this, and I'll let you read it." She wondered if she'd had a premonition. Is this why her memories of camp had been so present with her this morning?

As she read the obituary, she thought that probably a day hadn't gone by in the past thirty-four years that she hadn't thought about this man. And, at this moment, she was doing her absolute best to fight back a floodgate of tears.

She took a deep breath and walked to the overstuffed chair Ron had dropped into and where he was reading Sebastian Moore's *The Contagion of Jesus.* Momentarily she thought it was odd that Ron, on such a beautiful day, would be inside reading, but she let go of her concern. As she placed the paper in his lap, she said, "I think I'll start some lunch."

This was how Chris reacted to tough situations. For all of her life, she'd ignore the problem at hand as long as possible, busying herself, keeping occupied, getting to work. It was no different today. And referencing Scarlett O'Hara's famous line, she thought, *I'll think about this tomorrow.* But as she walked into the kitchen, she could no longer hold back the tears, the ones that until now she had been doing a good job of containing. They welled up in her eyes. Quickly she retreated to the bathroom and did her best to remember how to handle "crisis mode."

Flushing the toilet and running the water gave her adequate time to wash her face, refresh her lipstick, and return to the kitchen as if all was well. But she knew before the week was out she would be reflecting on the overwhelming impact Frederick Taylor had had on her life.

She entered the kitchen and assembled several chicken salad sandwiches, which she arranged on a platter with some chips and pickles. As she headed to the front porch, she yelled out to David, who was placing his fishing gear on the dock, "Lunch is ready."

His rapid response was, "Any chance we can eat out here on the dock?"

"That works for me. I'll send Ron out with lunch. Want a beer?"

"Sure," Dave said, as he pulled the Adirondack chairs into a semicircle.

As Chris walked back through the camp, she noticed that Ron was absorbed in the obituary.

"Mom, the man who died, Fred Taylor... It says he's survived by a son, Carl. Isn't he the kid you fell in love with here at the camp when you were a teenager? I remember when Greg and DeEtte were in their teens, you had a talk with them about short-lived summer romances."

"Yes, he is. I'm surprised you remember my sharing that," she said, forcing a laugh. "Your dad wants to eat lunch on the dock. Will you take this platter of sandwiches and grab him a beer?" Chris asked, buying some time. "I'll join you in a few minutes."

Ron did as instructed, and as she watched him approach the dock, she turned and walked to the pine bookshelves her dad had built under the staircase and found the camp photo album labeled "1950s." She pulled it from its place; walked to the large, oblong, pine dining room table her father had built so many years before; dropped into a chair; and opened the page labeled "August 1957."

CHAPTER 3

*A*nother August, and here we are ready to enjoy another week at camp, Chris had thought at age fifteen, as she sat in her one-piece blue bathing suit, shaving her legs. The blue porcelain pan, in which her grandmother had once bathed her, sat at her feet on the front porch. This basin, like many of the items Chris used and enjoyed here, were those Grandma Wright no longer needed or wanted. Over the years, that was the reason many of the things surrounding her had found their way to camp.

Her swift movements with the safety razor quickly removed the stubble from her underarms and tanned legs, which were shapely and toned. Although she was more than aware that no one had ever called her thin and trim, she sensed that for a teenager she possessed a nice body shape; at least that's what she saw reflected in the bathroom mirror after a shower. She had grown happy with the changes in her body that had been brought about with the onset of puberty, and she remembered the rite of passage that had occurred three years earlier when her periods had begun.

It hadn't been that long ago when her mother had come into her bedroom one cold November morning to make an announcement.

"Chris, are you awake?" she heard her mother whisper softly in her ear.

"Uh-huh," Chris murmured.

She could smell the Tabu, the perfume her mother always wore, as well as the tobacco on her breath.

"When you get up and get ready, after breakfast, I want you to walk down to the store. You know you're growing up, Chris, and I think it's time, young lady, that you started wearing a bra."

"OK," was all that Chris could think to say, as the news of her being a "young lady" floated around in her head.

"All right. I'll see you later," her mom said as she tiptoed out of the bedroom, where the pink-and-white-striped drapes were still drawn.

Chris had hoped her mother's whispers wouldn't waken Diane, her younger sister, whose twin bed was nestled in the opposite corner. Although the pink-print wallpaper, white vanity, and chair gave the large bedroom a girly look, the clothes tree on which Chris's dungarees and plaid shirt hung stood as a reminder of the outdoor wear she climbed into every day.

Sitting in the kitchen, she remembered the swirl of strange thoughts she had experienced that morning while sitting in the bathtub. She silently repeated the words her mother had whispered in her ear just an hour ago, "young lady." At times the growth spurts and physical changes she was experiencing mystified her. She wished she had a big sister to confide in like a few of her girlfriends did. But Chris knew she was strong enough to handle the changes; at least that's what she kept telling herself.

As she ate her hot oatmeal with some banana slices on top, the radio reported temperatures in the low thirties. Chris glanced out the window and smiled as she saw that the sidewalks were bare. She could forgo her boots.

It was a short walk to Dot's Dress Depot, where her mother, Mary, had worked since Chris's younger brother Hal had started kindergarten. The small shop was located on Main Street and appealed to female tourists and local professional women who taught at the school, worked at the hospital, or were clerks or secretaries for the businesses in Cooperstown's busy downtown. The store show-cased the latest fashions and featured selections for teenage girls, "junior miss"–style clothing.

It was always such a delight for Chris when her mother sur-prised her and Diane with something from the shop. Her discount made her purchases of specialty items a bit easier, and last Christ-mas she had surprised her daughters with dressy cardigan sweaters.

As Chris stood in front of the plate-glass windows of the dress shop, she took special note of the tall, thin mannequins. One was adorned in a burgundy wool suit; another wore a rust-colored sweater with gray wool slacks; and a third was bundled in a deep-green plaid winter coat gathered at the waist by a wide black-leather belt.

Maybe someday I can dress like that, Chris thought hopefully.

As she walked through the front door, she heard the familiar tinkle of the bell affixed overhead and saw her mom with some customers.

"How was your walk?" her mother asked her.

"Oh, it was fine. But it's pretty chilly and smells like snow is in the air," Chris reported, recalling what the weatherman on the radio had said earlier.

Two shoppers busied themselves looking through racks of fall and winter wear while Chris hung out looking at other clothing arrivals that were more to her liking. She couldn't help notice how attractive her mother looked, her midlength dark-brown hair neatly styled. Her mom stood five foot seven and always wore high heels to match her outfit, which today was a blue knit skirt and top. Chris was always proud to be seen with her mother, who now excused herself from the shoppers and returned to the counter to hand Chris two white bras.

Oh, my goodness! thought Chris.

"Christine, I want you to try these on to see if they fit. Call me if you need help. When you get the first one on let me know," her mother instructed with a smile and a twinkle in her eye.

Staring at the two white brassieres she held in her hand, Chris made her way to one of the two dressing rooms, hung her coat on a hook, and unbuttoned her green sweater. She placed it on the bench in the corner of the small space and thought, as she looked in the mirror, *Is this the last time I'll wear an undershirt?*

She quickly removed the white shirt and picked up one of the bras, realizing she needed to unhook it first. As she put it on, she found she couldn't get it hooked in back, so she figured she'd hook it in front. After swinging the garment around to the back, she raised it into place as she slipped her arms through the straps. This seemed like an awful lot of work, but she was pleased when she finally pulled the cups over her breasts.

"OK, Mom," yelled Chris.

An anxious mother stepped up to the room and pulled back the curtain. For the first time in her life, she observed her first-born in, as she later would share with her husband, her first piece of lingerie.

"I think that's a perfect fit, Christine. Try on the other one. It's the same size but a different style. Then decide which one you'd like to wear home. I'll cut off the tags and put the other one in a bag for you to take. OK? No more undershirts for you, young lady."

Those words again… "young lady," thought Chris.

The feeling of being a young woman was what Chris now thought about as she sat on the front porch of the camp. She was fifteen, almost grown up.

She tossed the soapy water from the basin onto the front lawn, if that's what you could call it. The area in her sight was covered with pine needles and tiny pinecones dropped from the towering balsams and firs that surrounded the cottage; a worn path led from the porch steps to the dock. Although there were many trees, the first of their branches were fifteen to twenty feet off the ground, so Chris easily could see Seventh Lake through the pine-sheltered space.

When the Wright family had arrived in the early afternoon the day before, they weren't disappointed that the weather forecast for the central Adirondacks—warm, dry, and in the low eighties for the second week in August—proved to be true. And so this morning, the first day of the week, Chris had risen early and joined her mom and dad at the kitchen table for fried eggs, toast, and coffee, then quickly donned her bathing suit.

With the leg shaving complete, Chris applied Coppertone to her legs, face, shoulders, and as much of her back as she could reach. After grabbing her towel and bathing cap, she ran down the porch steps and continued to the dock, where she left her towel and tucked her shoulder-length, dark-blonde tresses into the cap. She eased into the lake from the dock, noting that the water and air temperature were about the same—seventy degrees. After she swam the breaststroke to the raft, the one her dad had built several years earlier, she grabbed hold of the handy ladder.

She was grateful that her dad had placed it on the raft to help her get to the platform. She so wished that, like the men, she simply could pull herself up onto its surface, but to date Chris hadn't been able to master that.

As she was about to climb the ladder, she heard the sound of an outboard motor closing in on her. She watched as the Chris-Craft approached the raft, traveling far too fast. The young man at the helm must have seen Chris grasp the raft's gray wooden ladder to steady herself, because he immediately cut the engine. He'd come too close for safety, and the floating dock rocked with the pounding of the waves as Chris held on tight. When she turned her head, she saw the motorboat pull into the neighboring dock a hundred feet away.

Unsure who this guy was who had caused her early-morning discomfort, Chris, once she was atop the raft, settled into her routine of diving into the lake. As she stood to take her second dive, she turned and heard the splashing of water behind her. The young man she'd just seen recklessly driving the boat was swimming straight toward her. She didn't move. She stood like a high priestess staring down at a naughty invader.

Treading water, he looked up at Chris and said, "Sorry about the waves, but...is it OK if I come up?"

Surprised and unsure what to do, Chris heard herself say, "Sure."

In an instant the boy lifted himself out of the lake and onto the raft. With water streaming down his arms, legs, and torso, he now stood a few feet from her. His actions rocked the platform, and Chris, staggering a little, regained her footing and balance.

There was something about this boy that unsteadied her even more. He was tall, well built, and fair. She knew he was at least five or six inches taller than her five-foot-five frame. His brown hair was in a brush cut, and as he ran his hand over it, water sprayed everywhere.

"Hi. I'm Carl Taylor. I really apologize for the waves. My dad is always telling me to slow down on my approaches to the dock."

As the sun glistened off Carl's wet body, Chris was flooded with thoughts of how good-looking he was. He reminded her of Johnny Weissmuller, the star of the popular Tarzan movies. Carl was toned, muscular, and very attractive, and he gave the impression of being secure in himself. She liked his air of confidence and his full smile, revealing beautiful teeth. She thought of how nice it was to be greeted like this.

Back home she couldn't remember such an encounter with any of the local boys. Almost simultaneously they both said, "Maybe we should sit down."

In the back of Chris's mind, she thought, *How do I handle this situation? What do I say?*

When she had been in school plays, she relied on the drama teacher to call out directions, telling her where to stand, when to say her lines, how to move. She felt like she needed a director right now. She couldn't remember ever being in such a predicament—alone with a young man on a raft—wearing just a bathing suit and with no one else around.

As they sat down, Carl edged closer. Chris reflexively withdrew her leg when his arm grazed it as he moved into a position facing her. She was overwhelmed by how self-conscious she felt and relieved she had just shaved her legs. She removed her bathing cap and shook out her hair.

A little voice inside her head was whispered, *Calm down, Christine. You'll be fine. You can do this.* She tried to relax, yet she felt as if a million tiny ants were crawling around in her chest, an excitement she hadn't experienced before. It was new and frightening, but she thrilled at the feeling and wanted to sustain it.

"Is that your camp?" Carl inquired, glancing toward shore.

"Yes. It's called Lake Wrights, because our last name is Wright. I'm Christine," she added, "but everybody calls me Chris."

"Well, it's nice to meet you, Chris." His skin was drying in the sun and the clean air, and up close she could see a scar on his chin. "Are you here for the summer or just a week?"

"Just this week," she told him. "We arrived yesterday. We've been here most weekends this summer, but this is the only time my mom and dad take a week's vacation. What about you?"

"My parents rented the camp over there, the one with the tree stumps along the shoreline," Carl explained, as he pointed out the cottage a hundred feet south of the Wright camp. "We're here for just this week too, so it looks like we'll be seeing a lot of each other. I promise to be more careful with the boat. Maybe you'd like to go for a ride with me later."

Without second-guessing herself, she said, "I'd like that."

Carl smiled. "Great!"

What am I doing? Chris wondered. *Will Mom and Dad even let me go? They don't even know this guy, but he sure seems nice.*

As they basked in the morning sun, she became aware that Carl's eyes had glanced over her body more than once. For the first time, she remembered one of her mother's words—"attractive"—when she had spoken of how to appear in public.

I am attractive. He likes me, she thought. She loved the feeling that someone cared about her, and she sensed that Carl did. His deep-blue eyes sparkled, and she hoped that the smile radiating from those eyes was because of her. And so, in the morning sun with the air so clean and fresh, she decided to enjoy the moment for as long as it lasted. She felt her whole body relax.

Over the next hour, the two new acquaintances talked about their hometowns, their schools, sports, music, Elvis, the latest movies they'd seen, and the activities they enjoyed. The sun was intense on their bodies, and they periodically adjusted their positions. Once, when Carl tried to lie flat on his stomach, his hand touched hers, and she thrilled at the delightful sensations that filled her. It was hard for her to understand the queasiness she felt in the pit of her stomach or the goose bumps on her arms, which she hoped weren't apparent to Carl.

Their conversation continued, and Chris grew more comfortable. She ran her fingers through her hair, fluffing it, to assist the sun and the slight breeze in drying it. They talked and laughed at the stories they shared. She learned that Carl was sixteen, a year older than her; had a summer job until this week; and was an only child. His parents were both teachers in Cortland, New York, where they lived.

Without pad and paper, Chris was taking serious notes on this young man in the tan swimming trunks. She thought of the boys in town she'd walked home from school with, played with, and attended parties with, but they were nothing like this. This was different. Suddenly she felt mature, grown up. Why had she felt nervous, uneasy, and self-conscious? Was it because Carl's long, adoring glances hadn't gone unnoticed?

Chris, growing in confidence, gently asked, "Do you have a girlfriend back in Cortland?"

"I did. But once I got busy working this summer, she dumped me," Carl said with raised eyebrows and a shrug of his shoulders. "What about you, Chris? Going steady?"

"No. I've had lots of friends that are boys, but I've really never had a steady boyfriend."

"That's good," said Carl. "We can kind of start with a clean slate."

The heat of the sun continued to grow, as did this new friendship. Then, like a bunch of banshees, came the screams of Diane and Hal, Jr., as they raced off the front porch, ran to the end of the dock, and cannonballed into the water. They both swam to the dock and, once on top, had a ton of questions for the young man who was occupying their sister's attention. At first Chris was annoyed by their barging in, but then she was delighted as Carl, who seemed unfazed, tried to answer all their inquiries. "How come you're talking to my sister?" "Where do you live?" "Is that your boat?" She, too, was learning more about him.

Chris became the observer and learned much about the young man's demeanor and his seemingly kind and gentle personality as he responded to their interrogation.

Once their curiosity was satisfied, Hal and Diane dove back into the water and played around, leaving Chris and Carl alone once more. She wasn't quite sure where to go with the conversation and thought, *My God. I'm always talking to everyone. Why am I so tongue-tied?*

As the air became filled with the noise of seaplanes taking off and landing on the lake, the squeals and screams of Hal and Diane's splashing, and motorboats departing from nearby docks, Chris and Carl relaxed and discovered they felt even comfortable when their voices fell silent. More time elapsed; Chris didn't want this moment to end.

In time Chris, feeling more confident, expressed to Carl her pride in achieving her American Red Cross life-saving badge that summer.

"Up until last Friday," Carl said, "I was helping my dad and some of his friends paint houses. The pay was good, and it'll help when I go to college, but man, was it hot and dirty." He let out a groan and swiped his hand across his brow.

"I'll bet being here is a real vacation after what you've been doing," Chris speculated.

"You can say that again," he said, as he rose up on his elbows.

"Carl, are you out there?" a woman's voice called. "We're leaving in a half-hour."

Chris noticed a pleasant-looking woman with curly brown hair wearing blue slacks and a matching print blouse walk out onto the dock.

Carl yelled back, "I'll be right in, Mom."

I don't want him to go, Chris thought.

Carl turned to Chris and apologetically said, "I'd better go. We're driving up to visit my aunt and uncle and cousins for the day at their camp on Raquette Lake. We should be back after supper. Want to go out on the boat with me then?"

Is this a date? she wondered. Then she quickly responded, "I'd love to."

"See you then," Carl replied, as he dove into the water, rocking the raft once more and swimming to the neighboring dock. Upon arriving he turned, smiled, and waved good-bye to Chris.

Oh, good. It's not over. I'll see him later.

She lay back on the raft with her face to the glorious, blue sky above her. Her brother and sister were still swimming about in the lake, but it didn't keep Chris from a reverie she couldn't explain any more than her rapid heartbeat.

She had no idea how long she had been thinking of the upcoming evening when she heard her dad's voice from the dock.

"Chris, can you come on in and give me a hand with the trees?"

"Sure, Dad. I'll be right there," Chris replied, although she wished there was another choice. She didn't want to leave her daydreaming. Drawing her hair up to the top of her head, she caught it there and encircled it with a rubber band she had placed around her wrist earlier. She slid gently off the raft and was able to keep her dry hair as she swam gently toward shore.

"I'll be right with you, Dad, as soon as I put some clothes on," Chris yelled to an unseen father. He was out back, where Chris found him a few minutes later. She was now dressed and ready for work. She approached her dad, who was securing a log in a sawhorse. He picked up the two-man saw and, as he held out one end for Chris, asked, "Who was that young man I saw with you on the raft?"

She felt her face flush. She hadn't realized she'd been watched.

"He's vacationing with his folks in the next camp over from ours. He seemed really nice, Dad."

"It's all right, Chris. You don't have to explain. It's probably time you started seeing young men you like. You're at the age when you should start to date. These things happen, you know!"

With nothing more said, they went about their work. It seemed, to the satisfaction of her father, the matter of Chris and her new boyfriend had been addressed.

The rest of the late morning and early afternoon were taken up with Hal Wright sawing down evergreens that had been topped out by the wind over the past year and that he and Chris now sawed for firewood. She was grateful he wanted her to help him today; that didn't happen a lot lately. She watched her dad admiringly as he swung his ax, sweat dripping off his shirtless chest.

Chris loved hearing her dad's words—"Good job, Chris" or "Thanks for all your hard work." As her father's firstborn, Chris loved the special relationship she had with him. It made no difference that she was a girl; when he needed help, he always called on her to do whatever the task might be, and she felt proud to be asked. She wanted to be just like him.

Growing up she was a tomboy; her dad had called her that, as did most everyone at school. She had romped through Cooperstown in search of neat hiding places or uncovering hidden paths, creating a new trail down to the outlet, and playing along the streambed.

She often played with boys her age, returning to the playground after school, wearing her blue jeans. She stayed fit, perhaps from learning to outrun the bullies or being strong enough to shove back, which she often did. No one was going to push her around and get away with it. Her dad had convinced her that she could stand up against anyone.

She often walked the several blocks to the Wright Lumber Mill, where she was welcomed by her dad and grandfather, along with uncles and male friends she'd met over the years. She yearned to be like them—skilled, hardworking, and physically able to handle two-by-fours and four-by-sixes. She also wanted the knowledge her father possessed.

Her father's kind words fulfilled a need for her to receive his approval and admiration. She never heard her father say "I love you," but then she hadn't heard those words from her mother either. It didn't seem to matter; their actions more than made up for the lack of the spoken word. Chris never feared anything. She knew, without a doubt, that her folks always would be there to watch over, protect, and care for her.

These strong feelings of affection that swirled about in her mind were intensified as she thought about the new friendship she had forged with Carl Taylor. She already could hear *him* saying those three words—"I love you."

CHAPTER 4

Hours later, as the Wrights finished dinner, along with the warm apple kuchen her mother had made for dessert, Chris heard the sound of a motorboat in front of the camp.

A bit reluctant and unsure of the response she'd receive, Chris turned to her parents and said, "Carl, the boy next door who I met this morning, wants to take me for a ride on the lake. Can I go?"

"What do you think, Hal?" asked Mrs. Wright.

"That'll be fine, Chris," he responded. "You just tell him not to go speeding all over the lake, and you be home before dark. And tell him he's carrying precious cargo."

"Thanks, Dad," Chris said, relieved and thinking her dad's words would be a good conversation starter with Carl. She ran out the front door then slowed her pace as she walked to the dock.

After Chris jumped in, Carl gently eased the boat away and, without causing too much of a wake, headed swiftly across the water to the narrow channel that connected Sixth and Seventh Lake. Chris fondly recalled her first memory of passing under this bridge when she was eight.

Her dad once had said, "Chris, look down and let me know if you see the line at the bottom that separates the two lakes." She remembered her interest at peering down through the crystal-clear water, and although she could see clear to the bottom, there was no line she could detect. When Chris had told her father that she couldn't see any line, he had laughed and explained that just as he had made her look, someday she could try to pull this little prank on someone else.

Here's my chance, she thought, as they approached the channel. "Carl, have you seen the line at the bottom that separates Sixth Lake from Seventh Lake?"

"Really, there's a line?" As he slowed to the posted five miles an hour, he looked down. He eased the craft out from the under the bridge, then turned to Chris and smiled. "It's a joke, right?"

"Yep. My dad pulled it on me years ago. You're the first one I've gotten to fall for it."

Carl maneuvered the boat along the north shore of the lake and into the large bay then circled back. In their view two seaplanes sat at the end of the lake waiting for the next eager summer vacationers who wanted to explore by air the vastness of the awe-inspiring central Adirondacks and Fulton Chain of Lakes.

Returning down the lake, Carl guided the craft under the bridge and now cruised the north shore of Seventh Lake. It was Chris's favorite side, as the camps ceased to exist a third of the way along the shoreline and state land continued, providing a couple of lean-tos and several additional camping sites as the hardwoods and tall white pines sheltered the land to the end of the lake. More than once, as she canoed with her dad in their wooden craft, he quietly had said, "Look, Chris." And there, appearing from the cover of the forest, would be a deer or two drinking from the lake. It was the reason Chris, although she was certainly comfortable enjoying her present ride, thought a canoe was the best means of transportation on this lake, as she could explore the shoreline, tiny bays, and inlets on her own.

As they neared the beach, which was really nothing more than an island sandbar near the end of the lake, Carl slowed and dropped the anchor. He jumped into the water, which wasn't quite to his knees, and turned to reach his hand out to Chris. She readily took it as she stepped into the lake. As they waded to the sandy shoreline, Carl suggested they walk around the small island.

The walk was slow, neither one in a hurry. Chris gingerly stepped onto water-filled logs, doing a balancing act as she walked the length of each. Long ago the beach had been dotted with these logs, which the sun had bleached white.

Carl tried her one better, scaling to the top of a stump. It was fun; they weren't really showing off as much as seizing an opportunity to display their balance and physicality, and more important, to just have fun. They strolled along the water's edge, and as their bare feet sank into the sand, they bumped against each other on occasion, held hands once or twice, and touched as a gesture of approval of something one of them had said.

The brilliant orange daystar had settled for the evening, and the beach was now deserted when Chris suggested they return to camp. It wasn't that she had any desire to abandon this romantic place, but an inner voice spoke to her about not wanting to disappoint her folks. She remembered her father's words, "Be back before dark."

As the breeze blew through her hair, she wondered what she had done to deserve such an emotionally fulfilling evening. It was dusk when Carl gently eased the boat alongside the dock in front of his camp, suggesting he could walk her back from there. Chris saw his folks sitting on their front porch. His father shouted out, "Glad to see you're back safe and sound."

Carl responded with, "That we are, Dad. I'm going to walk Chris back to her camp."

As they walked down the dock, the smell of a campfire filled the air. When they neared the Wright property, it became apparent that Chris's dad had started a blaze in the fire pit near the shoreline. In their absence her family had gathered around the circle of stones and sat on logs and stumps, toasting marshmallows. Chris suggested that Carl join them.

"We do this a lot at camp," Chris said. "Dad builds the fire, and we roast marshmallows and listen to him tell deer stories. We've heard them a million times, but it's always fun to hear them again. He makes them sound so interesting."

After introductions were made, Carl joined the circle, placing a marshmallow on one of the available sticks and extending it into the flames. Everyone seemed happy, but Chris knew no one was happier than she.

That happiness continued over the next three days, as Chris and Carl managed an hour or two each afternoon or evening to take a short hike, play cards, paddle the canoe, or work at putting a puzzle together on the Wrights' dining room table.

Then came the last evening of the Wrights' vacation stay. Carl's mother and father invited Chris to accompany them for a drive into Inlet for dessert. As she and Carl licked their chocolate custard cones, they walked into the town park and stood watching, along with other visitors, the sun descend over Fourth Lake behind the distant mountains.

"This sunset is beautiful, Chris, just like you," Carl said, as he turned to her.

Did I hear him right? Chris wondered. *Did he say I was beautiful?* She was beside herself and, unsure how to respond, said a simple and soft, "Thank you."

As she was expressing herself, Carl heard his father's familiar yell announcing their return to camp. He took Chris by the hand. "I guess it's time to go."

"This has been absolutely lovely. I need to be sure to thank your mom and dad for bringing us into town. I had fun," Chris said, as she held on to his hand, making sure it wasn't too tight.

Upon their return, Carl walked Chris back to her camp, over what now had become a familiar route through the wooded lot that separated the two cottages. Chris already had mentioned to

Carl that the Wrights would be departing early the next morning, so they exchanged addresses as well as phone numbers.

They sat together on the front steps until ten thirty that last night; neither had the right words, and neither wanted to be the one to say good-bye. But Mary Wright's call for Chris to come in was Carl's signal to stand, lean forward, take Chris by the shoulders, and give her a kiss—their first. Their eyes met briefly, and then Carl was gone.

Chris wanted to shout out loud. She never had felt so alive. How could—or would—she tell her mother? She stepped through the front door of camp as a different person. She felt herself being transformed from a young girl into a woman.

What an exquisite feeling!

How could these memories of fifty-three years ago still create within Chris the emotions she had experienced so long ago? As she closely examined the photographs her mother had taken that August, she glanced toward the dock, where she saw David and Ron clinking their beer cans together, toasting someone or something. She knew she needed to finish this musing soon.

But right now her heart swelled with the emotions she remembered of her first love, the very deep emotions, the sense of awe and wonder she had felt, knowing someone loved her.

Carl would now be sixty-nine years old. As the only son, how was he coping with his father's death? She was raising questions for which she had no answers.

She returned her thoughts to the brief teenage romance she and Carl had shared. She remembered how they had started writing letters back and forth almost as soon as they had returned home. Carl had called soon after his senior year began with the hope that she would be his date for his senior ball later that year.

The correspondence continued as they shared their daily routines and their involvement in clubs and church activities.

Chris was happy to report she had been elected president of both her Catholic youth organization as well as the school debate team and had been chosen to serve as the assistant editor of the school newspaper. Carl wrote about being a running back for his Cortland football team and said he would continue to serve as an officer for the student council and Key Club. There was always so much to say in their weekly Sunday telephone calls. Chris would follow up with a letter written on Monday and mailed on Tuesday. She loved writing letters to Carl.

The first week in December, Carl called and invited her to spend a few days at his house during Christmas vacation. Chris responded with excitement.

"Oh, Carl, I'd love to, but I'll need to talk to my folks about it. I'll let you know when I write this week. OK?"

"I hope so. It'll be great getting together again," Carl said happily.

But Chris never had the opportunity to mail her letter to Carl with the Wrights' approval. The next evening, just after the family had enjoyed a chicken and dumpling dinner, Mrs. Wright answered the ringing telephone in the foyer.

"It's for you, Chris." Dishtowel in hand, Chris walked into the foyer, where her mom handed her the receiver and softly said, "It's a man."

Chris remembered the man's words exactly. "Is this Christine Wright?" When she responded in the affirmative, the voice said, "This is Mr. Taylor, Carl's father." He spoke pleasantly but sternly. "Carl made a mistake, Chris, when he invited you to our house for Christmas. I'm not sure you know that we're Methodists, but there's no way Carl's mother and I want to see him get serious with a Catholic girl. We've talked to Carl about this, and he agrees, so there will be no more phone calls or letters. Do you understand?"

Chris knew she had no choice but to say, "Yes."

Mr. Taylor ended with a simple, "Thank you and good-bye."

She heard the click at the other end of the line but continued to hold the receiver. *This can't be happening*, she thought. The conversation had been so one-sided, so short; she knew Mr. Taylor had to have worked this out in his head in advance because there was such an economy of words.

She slowly replaced the receiver; her body shook as waves of grief flowed over her. "This can't be happening," she said out loud. "This isn't right. How can he do this?"

As she headed back to the kitchen, it was obvious to her mother that something was the matter, as she saw the tears running down her daughter's cheeks. Using the dishtowel as a handkerchief, Chris sat down at the kitchen table. Heaving and sobbing she shared the painful phone conversation with her mom.

In the days and weeks that followed, nothing could cheer Chris up, not even the coming of Christmas. The Wright family's annual trek to the farm just outside of town to cut their Christmas tree, usually a highlight for Chris, seemed routine. Decorating the house with Diane seemed more like work than delight. And when her mom handed Chris the bag of pinecones that she herself had collected that summer at camp, she kept her handkerchief handy as she dabbed her eyes and blew her nose while trying to be creative in assembling the cones and red ribbon in a basket for the foyer.

Many times she replayed the phone conversation in her head, questioning whether she should have asked to speak to Carl. She asked herself, *Why didn't you tell Mr. Taylor you didn't believe him about Carl's true feelings?* What she did know was that she was full of rage and hated Mr. Taylor.

She was in a state of disbelief and had hoped her mother would have been more sympathetic. But Mrs. Wright, after hearing Chris retell the phone conversation with Mr. Taylor, also was angry.

"It's probably best for you that it happened this way, Christine," her mother had said crisply. "You don't want anything to do with people who feel this way about Catholics. You need to get over it."

What Chris wanted right then was not "Get over it," but her mother's shoulder to cry on. But that didn't happen, and neither her mother nor father ever asked about Carl Taylor again.

Where was the love and comfort she so desired from her mother? As they stood admiring the fully decorated twelve-foot Christmas tree, Chris turned to her mother with tears in her eyes and asked once again, "Why, Mom? Why?"

"We both know the answer to that, don't we, Christine? If Carl and his family feel that way about our family, why would you want anything to do with them? There are some really nice boys in your class. Think about them, and take your mind off of Carl," Mary Wright insisted.

Though Chris would grow up and move on with her life, she clung to sweet memories of her brief romance with Carl. She had envisioned herself in her wedding dress and fantasized about the honeymoon, their first apartment, and the children that would make them a family. Now the only thing she felt, alone in her sorrow, was the heartache of knowing that all her hopes and dreams never would come to pass.

CHAPTER 5

"Mom, are you going to join us?"

Chris heard the shout from Ron and realized she needed to put the album back in its place, put herself back into the present moment, and reconnect with her husband and son.

She ran her hand gently over the black-and-white photographs in the vintage album, as if to reconnect with them. There were only six photos recalling that summer vacation of 1957, and to Chris, they looked as new and fresh as when her mom had snapped them. Chris always would be grateful for the three that included Carl and her in his motorboat and on the Wrights' dock. Almost wishing she could stay lost in the fifties, she rose tentatively from the wooden captain's chair at the end of the dining table. She walked slowly to the shelves across the room and put the album back in place.

As she strolled to the dock, she knew she was delaying the inevitable, putting off to a later time the issue she needed to address, the memories she needed to confront of Frederick Taylor. But she had a whole week at camp to think about it. Right now lunch was waiting on the dock.

She joined David and Ron, who were pretty well finished with their sandwiches, and heard Ron, between sips of beer, and still apparently preoccupied with the obituary, ask his father, "Dad, did you know this man?"

As Chris sat down in an Adirondack chair, David gave her an inquiring glance as she entered their space. Only learning now of

Fred Taylor's passing from Ron, David couldn't be sure just how much Chris already had shared and didn't want to say any more than she would want.

Again Ron made strong eye contact with Chris. She turned to him and said, "This was obviously a long time before your dad came into my life, Ron. I know that over the years I've talked about the Taylor family, especially my romance with Carl. Your grandmother took photos that summer. In fact that's where I was just now, looking at them. I couldn't remember if Mr. Taylor was in any of them, but I didn't think so. And I was right. He wasn't," she said quite emphatically. "It was just our family and three pictures of me and Carl. I have great memories of that summer."

David looked relieved that the burden of trying to answer Ron had now been removed, and Ron appeared to be satisfied with the responses. They all finished lunch as David flipped the tab on a can of beer. As he handed it to Chris, he said with a chuckle, "I guess this'll be a one beer lunch for me." They all settled back, enjoying the warmth of the sun and the laughter of happy vacationers that floated across the lake.

In times past it would have been normal for Chris to think, *God's in his heaven, and all's right with the world.* She often thought that being in this place was an experience of the world that couldn't get any better. But today was different. *This place is so beautiful and peaceful,* she thought. *If only my heart and soul could radiate this peace and tranquility.* Her insides felt tied in a knot.

Although a day didn't go by without Chris thinking of the secret she never had shared with anyone except David and her spiritual director, Father Jim, it hadn't consumed her as it did at this moment. How had she let herself keep the truth from being revealed? Lost in her thoughts, she stared at the shimmering surface of the lake.

Returning to the camp to wash the lunch dishes, she left the men to fish away their Saturday afternoon. She went about her work like a woman driven. She tidied rooms; she dusted; she found a myriad of chores to occupy her time.

Standing in the kitchen wringing out a sponge, and her to-do list now complete, she glanced at the clock and noted it was nearing four, her usual time for prayer. She retreated to one of the chairs on the back deck, where the fragrance of the balsam and pine enveloped her. Shortly she was greeted by a chipmunk that, after sniffing around and finding no nuts, scampered into the woods. The place was quiet and serene, and she meditated.

It was a little before five when David stepped onto the porch, interrupting Chris's prayer.

"We'll have to put off cocktails for a bit. Ron wants to celebrate Mass first. Is that OK with you?"

"Sounds great."

As Chris rose from her chair, David took her into his arms. "Chris, you need to know that in addition to the news about Fred that you're dealing with, Ron is also trying to work through some of his own issues. We need to be sensitive to that."

Chris, surprised by David's statement, asked, "What issues?"

David briefly shared that Ron had asked him if it was natural for a man to question his life choices—in his case the priesthood, celibacy.

"We talked briefly, Chris. I told him that in the early years of my first marriage, with a wife and young children, I questioned whether I had made the right choice. But through prayer and simply loving my family, I knew I had. Perhaps Ron's got the seven-year itch. He's only thirty-three. There's still time for him to marry and have a family, if that's what he's thinking."

Although shaken by the revelation, Chris entered the cabin with her emotions in check. "Dad says we're putting off cocktail hour," she reaffirmed, as she found her son clearing off the dining room table. "Let me change out of these work clothes and clean up a bit. Do you want me to set up the altar, or do you want to do it?"

"I'll do it, Mom. Get ready! Mass in five minutes."

Chris gave herself a quick sponge bath; then, wetting her hands, she proceeded to puff out her matted hair. Wrapped in a beach towel, she entered her bedroom and quickly chose a red-striped top and pair of white capri pants. As she stared into the mirror affixed to wall over the dresser, she asked herself, *How many women are as blessed as I am? I'm physically well at my age, and I have a son who's a priest and about to celebrate Mass for my husband and me at our camp.*

Glancing at the framed print of the Sacred Heart on the wall she uttered, "Thank you, Lord." She remembered the words she often had heard her spiritual director, Father Jim, repeat, *If the only prayer we ever utter is "Thank you," it would be sufficient,* and she repeated the words, "Thank you." She was now ready; as she reentered the living room, she realized David and Ron were too.

Ron, in his eighth year since ordination, had, as usual, brought his Mass kit in its black leather case, the gift she and David had given him the Christmas before he was ordained. Her son was wearing his vestments; it wasn't unusual that he'd brought them along with him. The dining room table, now covered in Grandma Wright's linen tablecloth, held candles, a cross, altar cloth, a chalice, wine, water, and hosts upon the paten.

"Are you ready, Mom?" Ron asked. "Would you like to lead us in an opening hymn?"

Chris led them in the first verse of "Praise to the Lord" as Ron positioned himself, facing his parents, behind the altar. Chris and David stood close by, responding when appropriate. David proclaimed the readings and psalm. Chris sang out, "Alleluia!" as she stood up next to David. Ron said, "A reading from the Gospel According to Luke."

As he read, Chris listened closely to the words from Chapter Twelve on this, the Nineteenth Sunday of Ordinary Time. "Be ready. You know not the day or the hour…" Ron recited.

As Chris and David sat down, Ron offered a three-minute reflection on the words of Luke.

Chris wondered, *Did Fred Taylor know his death was imminent? Did his death come suddenly? Did he have time to reflect on his life as he prepared to meet his maker?*

Stop daydreaming, Chris, she reprimanded herself, as Ron continued his homily. She always was impressed with Ron's ability to speak publicly. Rarely did he require his message to be written down. He was able to formulate his thoughts and speak in perfect sentences, getting his point across in just a few minutes. Even the diocese of Syracuse, where Ron served as a pastor, had recognized his aptitude for giving presentations and homilies, and other churches frequently called on him to lead parish retreats and evenings of reflection.

With the Mass of Anticipation said, David exited to the kitchen to prepare some drinks while Ron made his way upstairs to disrobe. The scent of extinguished candles filled the room as Chris carefully placed the sacred vessels away and folded the tablecloth. She always felt privileged not only to serve the church as Eucharistic minister and lay lector but also to have the opportunity to handle the sacred vessels. "That's the nearest I'll ever get to being a priest," she'd often say with a chuckle.

She stored the items and thought of Ron's sensitivity when, during the Prayers of the Faithful, he had asked God to take into his care the soul of Frederick Taylor.

If only he knew what transpired between him and me so many years ago. Chris had stopped herself from gasping out loud, yet again, when Ron had invoked Fred's name. Ron also had mentioned his grandfather and grandmother by name. "And let us pray for Hal and Mary Wright, that they continue to feel our love and know our gratitude for all they gave us—family, faith, and this great camp."

The next few days at camp became the family-centered retreat, where comfort and silence allowed each of them to read, sleep, swim, fish, hike, sip on a beer whenever they wanted, and gather for a barbecue with shared memories and laughter—a lot of laughter.

Their conversations and enjoyment of one another's company continued as they drove to Blue Mountain Lake and visited the Adirondack Museum. They hiked around Moss Lake, and they drove to Old Forge to watch a first-run movie. Their vacation week was wonderful, yet Chris still struggled with unresolved issues that her daily meditation didn't seem to alleviate.

She sensed the same was true for Ron. And just as she didn't want outside interference into her problem solving, she didn't meddle into Ron's. She lovingly provided him time and space.

CHAPTER 6

The restlessness that had plagued Chris since she first had arrived at camp had escalated. Even with her best "keep busy" efforts, the daily camp adventures, and her prayer, her heart and soul felt far from peaceful. There was simply no way, on this last full day of vacation, that she could sit in silence.

Canoe! That's what I'll do, she decided, as if a lightbulb had illuminated in her head. She could see herself smoothly gliding along Seventh Lake and was confident it was exactly what she needed—the peace and calm. Yes!

After grabbing her hat, as well as a life jacket off a hook on the front porch, she shared her plan with the men, who were fishing off the end of the dock. Chris slipped out of her comfortable brown sandals, donned the orange life preserver, and climbed into the cedar canoe as David untied the rope that secured it to the dock.

"I'll be back in an hour," she proclaimed.

As Chris paddled in the bright afternoon sun, her Filson hat shielded the heat and glare from her head and her sensitive hazel eyes. She paddled forward down the lake, her thoughts moving backward in time, not only to the memory of craving solitude, but also to the realization that she always isolated certain experiences, ideas, and thoughts inside herself. She thought of it as personal protection, a way to guard herself against the judgment of others.

With the physical exertion she was putting forth, she knew this was hardly the ideal still and silent space for prayer. It didn't lend itself to allowing her to slip into that dark hole deep within.

The dark hole...it seemed so foreboding, lonely and unwelcoming. Yet when Father Jim had suggested she make an effort to go to such a place mentally, she gave it a try. She would imagine herself as a seed in the deep, dark earth of midwinter. She came to understand that this was where new life begins, much like a baby in its mother's womb, being nourished by something not of its making, surrounded by all that could produce new life.

For Chris the imagery of the seed in the dark and cold ground worked. It was the place she always sought in daily meditation, the place of a created nothingness where she found her creator. She had long struggled to remove barriers that had prevented her from entering that inner realm. Today was no different. Typically a mantra, inspirational readings, or lines from Scripture allowed her to slip off earthly bonds and mentally move to a distant place. Today nothing was breaking down the barriers, absolutely nothing.

She paddled; she struggled; she paddled; she prayed. Then suddenly the words came, powerful and to the point. *Isn't the real question, Chris, why you've been lying to yourself all these years?*

The force of those words made as great an impact as if she'd been hit upside the head with a two-by-four. Momentarily she withdrew the paddle from the crystal-clear water. *I can't go there,* she thought. *I won't.*

Her paddle gently returned to its rightful place, and she maneuvered the craft into the narrow and shallow bay where Wheeler Creek flowed into the lake. Then she nudged the craft as far as possible. As often as she had canoed this lake over the years, she hadn't paddled up this creek since her youth. It was a special place, one she often thought of as having discovered herself. How many years ago had it been? Fifty-plus?

At age thirteen, when many of her friends had worried about suntans and reading fan magazines on their docks, she loved exploring, being the risk taker. She gingerly had navigated this same canoe around stumps and through downed pines and reached a point where travel was no longer possible. Today was no different. With two more paddle strokes, Chris wedged the canoe between a couple of large rocks at the edge of a small pine embankment.

Balancing herself, she stepped from the canoe, her bare feet touching the rocky bottom in a mere six or seven inches of water. The canoe wasn't going anywhere, and she was ready to leave behind her cares and concerns and just be alone.

The carpet of pine needles under the trees cradled her feet gently, in contrast to the creek bed. This solitary space was warm, and the afternoon sun enhanced the fragrance she had grown accustomed to here in the mountains: pine, balsam, and hemlock. The sun's rays streamed through the branches, creating a cathedral-like appearance. She stood frozen in time and space. Isolated.

As much as she loved David, throughout their marriage she always had sought out time and space to be on her own. Finally, after a day of wrestling with her thoughts and fears, she had arrived in an old and familiar place. It was like discovering treasure from long ago—buried away and now rediscovered—where she could just be.

As a child she had enjoyed pretending and had read much about the Native Americans of the Adirondacks. When hiking or paddling, she often had thought herself as a young Indian brave traversing the area perhaps a century or two earlier. She sensed that he would have been in pursuit of fish or game, maybe a pelt from a mink or beaver—not on a pleasure trip but one of survival. Her arrival at this spot so many years ago had placed her amid downed limbs and branches, where she had erected a teepee.

Where exactly did I build it? Chris now wondered as she searched for evidence from long ago. *If that framework were still here,* she thought, *I could crawl into it and pray.* Now all that appeared in her view was a carpet of needles upon which lay decaying logs and branches. She did come upon a small open area devoid of tree limbs and decided to simply sit down, Sitting Bull style.

As she sat she recalled when, as a twelve-year-old, she had escaped the grownups at the lumber mill and joined her male cousins out back. Makeshift swings had been fashioned with ropes suspended from the limbs of maple and oak trees. It was an impressive grove of old timber that stood guard over the lumber mill, and Chris had explored its trees since early childhood. She had an intimate relationship with each one, having climbed them over and over. She had sat high among the branches with the birds, allowing the leaves to camouflage her presence. Standing on the old wooden crates that the boys had stacked at the base of the trunk, she'd reach for the nearest limb then find enough traction between the bottom of her sneakers and the bark to successfully reach the lowest branch. Often she climbed up and out onto the limbs, declaring that it was like hiding in plain sight. And she also learned the simplicity and elegance of the branches, which allowed for a perfect perch for her to ponder the world around her; it was form and function at its best.

That was how she felt at the moment; she was in the perfect hiding place.

Suddenly the stillness enveloped her as it had so many years earlier when she had enjoyed this solitude from her treetop perch. She missed that isolation. There was something special about being alone in a place no one else had discovered and where no one knew you were—a secret abode where you could create your own world and where you were on your own. You could think your own thoughts, keep your own secrets.

As the lengthening shadows of the surrounding trees bathed her, she closed her eyes and thought, *Don't I already know what needs to be done? Why is it so hard for me to admit that as a "good Catholic girl" I sinned? That I had sex with a married man? After thirty-four years, I've almost begun to believe the lies I've told myself. What am I so afraid of?*

She twinged slightly as her inner voice responded, *The truth, Chris. The truth.*

"It was so long ago," she whispered out loud. Slowly, amid the moss-covered logs in this peaceful place, with all of creation surrounding her, she let go of her stronghold on that week in August 1976 and surrendered to the memories.

CHAPTER 7

It's all about the lake, Chris thought, as she paddled the old wooden canoe down Seventh Lake through the early-morning fog on what she thought was a pretty typical morning in August 1976.

But then, as she had discovered over the years, were any two days ever the same in the Adirondacks? Although the fog was lifting, the sky appeared ominous. Nevertheless, with only a week's vacation time to spend at the family cottage, she wanted to take every opportunity to canoe, under her own power, down the lake. So she had pushed off from the dock an hour before, at seven, when the lake was mirror-like. Except for a pair of loons, she was the only other thing slicing through its silvery surface.

Not much had changed on Seventh Lake in the decades since she'd been coming here, and for this she was grateful. Those days of her youth were dimming in her memory, and yet the girl from those days was still very much alive inside her. Now a woman of thirty-four, she still delighted in the feel of the old cedar canoe her father had kept seaworthy all these years. She took pleasure in the fact that maintaining good physical health allowed her to enjoy this early-morning regimen without much effort. And she was grateful for that too, because if the sky continued to threaten, she might have to hightail it back to camp.

She recalled those days in the mid-1950s when, without asking her parents, and without her parents having any worries, she simply pushed the canoe into the waters of Seventh Lake and made her way down its shoreline. She found it interesting that in those youthful, innocent days, even though she considered herself a good swimmer, she never paddled more than forty or fifty feet from the shore—more often a comfortable thirty feet. She still kept to that same route and maintained the same distance from the docks, which appeared every hundred feet or so.

After the far-from-normal year Chris had just experienced, Seventh Lake provided her a familiar routine and comfortable surroundings.

She recalled that when she was a new bride living in Clinton, New York, a year out of college, she could drive from the couple's apartment to the family camp in just two hours. She questioned why she hadn't come more often. She knew that her marriage to Mike had had an impact on that. Mike was good-looking and athletic, someone who exercised outdoors regularly. Whenever Chris suggested a trip north for the weekend, Mike, more times than not, concocted a reason they couldn't go. After the third or fourth time, Chris understood that the Wright camp wasn't a place he enjoyed or felt comfortable visiting; perhaps in the 1960s, as he hadn't grown up with kerosene lamps or the use of an outhouse, it was just too unfamiliar and uncomfortable for him. On his few visits, he had helped his father-in-law carry wood and haul the boats to the dock, all without complaint, but Chris could detect that this wasn't an environment to which he adapted easily.

By contrast, since Chris was eight years old, a year hadn't passed that she hadn't embraced the camp environment. This year, 1976, was no different, except she wasn't wearing a wedding band.

A breeze had increased in intensity, and steel-gray clouds descended suddenly and powerfully. The first huge drops hit her knees and nose. Her blouse billowed in the wind.

As she headed for Lake Wrights, she clung to the thoughts of her ten-year marriage, which had withered and finally ended last year. Chris frequently thought that her biggest regret was that it had produced no children. Although the state Supreme Court had made the divorce official nine months earlier, she felt the marriage wouldn't be dissolved until the annulment was completed. And that decree had been issued just a few weeks ago. Her mom and dad, sensitive to the emotion and stress Chris had endured the previous year, had suggested she take some time alone at the camp; they would delay their annual trek to Seventh Lake and join her at week's end.

Over the past two years, Chris and Mike had shared many conversations about their separation. Chris, in her head, often described it as "weird." How was it that she hadn't guessed him to be gay? Why hadn't she questioned the amount of time he had spent with Tom? Yes, they were both professors in the sociology department at a quasi–Ivy League college, but what did she know? Maybe this much conferring and consultation was necessary for their class preparations and the occasional papers they wrote jointly.

Whatever the case, it was only after Mike had moved into the Victorian home Tom occupied on Green Street, just a couple of blocks from their apartment, that Chris realized how naive she had been. That first week, after rumors began to fly through the small, tight-knit community, she finally said to herself, *You fool.*

At times she felt she had been hit by an eighteen-wheeler. She called herself everything she could imagine—"stupid," "dumb," and "blind."

Perhaps the toughest part came when she first shared her dilemma with some close friends and no one seemed surprised.

How embarrassing is that? was all she could think. In fact a few said, "Really, Chris? Didn't you know?"

She felt so foolish—a grown woman who apparently couldn't see any handwriting on the wall or, if she did, chose to ignore it. And that was what she prayed about the most—her strong desire to do just about anything to make her marriage succeed.

When the annulment had been finalized, and Mike had removed the last of his possessions from their apartment, Chris called to ask him if they could have lunch at one of their favorite restaurants.

After a year or two of daily meditation and asking herself the same questions, she decided to ask Mike if he would explain why he had kept her in the dark when he knew he was gay. Mike, who still thought of Chris as his best friend, softly and almost tenderly shared his growing-up years, when he first had come to an understanding of his sexuality. He didn't want to disappoint his parents and thought if he got married he'd be OK. He knew he loved Chris and thought he'd get over it.

"I'm truly sorry, Chris, but my getting over it obviously didn't happen," he told her.

In the days that followed, more than once Chris had said to herself, *What a sham!* She wanted an out, an escape. When her mom and dad had suggested she take some time alone at camp, she thought it the perfect opportunity for a retreat to Lake Wrights.

Here she was, a free woman, afloat on Seventh Lake, with no responsibilities except for her job. *Not bad for a thirty-four-year-old,* she thought. Or was it?

She was a successful journalist and freelance writer and had won the respect of her peers. Without children she had immersed herself in civic and professional organizations and was heading up the community's bicentennial celebration this year. She told herself she was happy but often shared with Father Jim that she felt unfulfilled.

The sky grew dark, the rain pellets striking her body with more intensity. Chris saw the first flashes of lightning and remembered how she had handled the emotional storm that had encircled her for the past eighteen months; she realized how much easier it was to deal with nature. The thunder rattled off the mountains. She extended her upper body as she moved the paddle from side to side.

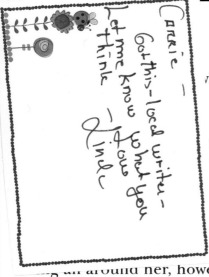

whipping through the trees; the waters a bit more muscle into her strokes, moving another lightning bolt lit up the sky. breaking loose. The rain came in torrents. ed down her cheeks, she recalled the never-ending tears—that had rained go. This morning's powerful rain was also surprisingly cleansing. She arched ed, "Bring it on!" With lightning crashing all around her, however, she knew better than to be out on the water.

Only twenty feet from the shoreline, she thought of pulling in at any one of the docks she was passing, when she heard a man's voice yell, "Over here! Get off the lake."

Across the lake, a flash of lightning was instantaneously followed by the clap of thunder. Too close for comfort. Pelted by rain, Chris made out a man, just ahead to the left of her canoe, descending the wooden steps of an open porch. She pulled the canoe alongside the dock, where a gray-haired stranger grabbed the rope from the stem of the canoe and tethered it. Chris, now dripping wet, took the man's extended hand as he pulled her up and onto the dock.

"Get up on the porch," he shouted, as he grabbed her paddle.

He followed Chris to the shelter of the covered porch. The thunder and lightning continued.

"Let me get you a towel. And how about a cup of coffee?" he said in a single breath. He departed into the interior of his cabin, not waiting for a response. In seconds he reemerged, handing her a large blue towel, which she used to wipe her face and run swiftly over her wet hair and body. Soaked and totally exhausted, she sank into a metal folding chair. It was only when her rescuer handed her the mug of hot coffee that she recognized him. *Oh, my God,* she thought. *It's Carl's father.*

Before she could say anything, he offered, "Wasn't sure how you take your coffee, so I did a sugar and milk. That's how my wife takes it, so thought I'd do the same for you."

Chris took a long sip from her cup as Frederick Taylor sat down in a similar chair a few feet away. He had aged, but the nineteen years since she had last laid eyes on him had been kind. He reminded her of Carl.

Chris thought, *Is this how Carl looks as an adult? Funny, I don't remember him looking that much like his dad back then.*

But now, as she sized him up, she was reminded of the yearbook photograph Carl had sent her in the fall of his senior year. Nineteen years later she still had it tucked away in a wooden keepsake box with the cards and letters he had sent. Carl had let his hair grow out from the summer brush cut, and by the time the photo was taken, it was nicely styled. There certainly was a strong resemblance between Carl and the man who sat before her, the man she had hated for so long.

"Is this how you planned to get your morning shower?" he said, turning to Chris with a smile.

"Not really, but at least it's warm."

The chair was comfortable and the coffee enjoyable, and she was grateful to be off the lake. As both kept their eyes facing forward, they watched the torrents of rain pour down and drip off the edge of the porch roof. Trying to be inconspicuous, Chris glanced over at the man, whom she had grown to despise, and offered, "Thank you for the rescue and the coffee. It's very good."

He didn't seem to recognize her, and she pondered, just for a minute, if she should keep him in the dark.

Chris always had hated practical jokers and anyone not leveling with her. Ironically, she often said that she loved the truth, and today she wasn't about to play games.

Finally she asked, "Do you remember who I am?"

"Should I?" came the response from the attractive midfifties man.

As his blue eyes caught hers, she noticed he was glancing at the front of her blouse. Chris only now realized it was soaked and had become transparent. It clung to her, and his eyes became riveted on her firm breasts. She placed her mug down long enough to casually reach for the towel beneath her, pretending she needed to dab at her hair. She continued to hold the towel in front of her.

"I'm Chris Wright. Remember nineteen fifty-seven? Carl's girl-friend? The romance you put an end to?"

Seemingly at a loss for words, Fred Taylor extended his arm, placed his empty coffee cup on the porch railing, and took a long look at Chris. She was unsure of where to take the conversation. And she didn't need to. He balled his right hand into a fist and tapped it against his lips. Head slightly bowed, he said, "You know, Christine, it was a different time, and I thought differently about religion—and frankly a lot of things—back then. I was very involved in my church and sat on a leadership council. I wasn't going to risk being removed because my son was going to marry a Catholic. That was almost twenty years ago. So much has changed since then. I know my thoughts and attitudes certainly have since I made that phone call to you. I'm sorry."

Chris was hearing his words, but his face showed no signs of remorse. There was a momentary pause before he continued. "From the sound of your voice, I'm getting the impression that you've been holding on to a lot of anger for a lot of years."

"You bet I have," Chris said. "I still can't believe how cruel you were. I never believed that Carl wanted to end our relationship. I always knew it was about what you wanted. Did you have any idea how Carl and I felt about each other?" She felt her anger rise and a tightening in her being.

"Chris, again I'm sorry. What else can I say?"

She sat in silence, sipping on her coffee and glancing out at the lake. She pondered his words, *What else can I say?*

She recalled her recent conversations with Mike, musing, *Everyone lives their lives and makes their decisions, and even when others are affected and hurt by them, in the end what else is there to say? Mr. Taylor makes it sound so simple. "I'm sorry." I'd like to hit him over the head with a baseball bat.*

She looked out at the rain, thought about his words, and wondered why, of all people, he had to be the one to rescue her from the storm. Finally she uttered, with some difficulty, "Your apology is accepted. But you need to know that I can forgive, but I can never forget what you said and how you ended our relationship." There was a period of silence, and finally Chris asked, "Can you tell me about Carl?"

With Chris changing her focus, they both seemed to relax a little.

Fred replied, "Well, he's still the great guy you remember. He graduated from high school and went on to graduate from college. He studied business and accounting. He became a certified public accountant and works for a firm in Cortland, where he lives with his wife and my two granddaughters, Kim and Susie. I think he's pretty happy and has a good life. And what about you?"

For the next half-hour, and over a second cup of coffee, Chris shared bits and pieces, a brief distillation of the past two decades— the failed marriage and no children. However, she perked up when describing several trips abroad and her writing career—the freelance articles that had been published and her daily column, "Around Town," that she wrote for the *Herald and Courier.* She also mentioned David, the reporter she'd known for years and was now dating.

"Do you love him?" Fred asked.

"Yes, very much. He's a wonderful man, a widower with two young children. We've talked about marriage, but we aren't quite there yet in our thinking, or I should say, I'm not. Just coming out of a failed marriage, I'm a little gun-shy of jumping into another so soon after my divorce and annulment."

Fred probed Chris about what exactly an annulment was and how it was different from a divorce. She explained in simple terms the ability of a Catholic person to remarry in the Church after having been married once in the Church and going through a divorce.

"It's sort of the Church's version of a good seal of approval," Chris offered.

"So it sounds to me like you're single again and able to check out the field of men out there."

"That's really not my style," Chris quickly retorted. "I don't need to go searching. I know the kind of man I want. I'm pretty certain, at this point, that David fits that bill."

"Just remember, Chris, once you're married, you're married for a long time," Fred instructed.

Grateful that the morning storm was gone as quickly as her cup of coffee, Chris sensed the need to move on. The sky was turning blue with mounds of puffy, white, cumulus clouds. She rose to leave and asked, "Is Mrs. Taylor here?"

"She will be on Friday. She's in Baltimore this week at an English teachers' conference. We've rented this place for two weeks, so I've got a jumpstart on a little R and R. This is the first time we've rented on Seventh Lake since that year you remember. We usually stay with my brother on Raquette Lake, but he's got a full camp these coming weeks, so we decided to settle here."

"Well, enjoy your stay," was all Chris could offer. "And thanks again for the rescue and the coffee." Chris handed the wet towel and empty mug to Mr. Taylor, who by now had insisted she call him "Fred" and drop the "Mister." She grabbed the damp paddle that leaned against the rail and headed for the dock, where steam rose off the boards as the intense morning sun did its best to dry it out.

"If you come by tomorrow, I'll have the coffee ready," Fred offered, as he walked Chris to the dock.

"I may do that," she replied, without any thought of actually following through.

Do I really need to deal with this man again?

As she waved good-bye and paddled down the lake, she considered how strange and coincidental this morning had been. *What were the chances of winding up on Fred Taylor's front porch?* she asked herself. If Fred hadn't broken up the relationship between her and Carl, it was very possible that he might have wound up being her father-in-law, and right now they might all be at Lake Wrights on vacation—she and Carl with their children, and Mr. and Mrs. Taylor with them. She thought how strange the prospect of that was. Then, realizing how fruitless the daydream was, she let it go.

As she paddled, she reflected on Fred Taylor and saw in her mind's eye an adult Carl. The size and shape she remembered of Carl she saw in his father. Their voices were similar, and their smiles created dimples in their cheeks. Their deep-blue eyes were identical. *But Carl never had that cynical streak I heard in his father's voice that sad day,* she thought.

Chris brought the canoe to shore and turned it over to let out the water that had been sloshing about in the hull. That complete, she walked up the steps to camp, dropped out of her clothes just inside the door, and put on her bathing suit. She retreated momentarily to hang the wet clothes on the line her dad had strung years ago between two pines on the side of the cottage. Moments later, with the duff wiped off her feet, she brewed her own small pot of coffee. She took the cast iron skillet down from its hook and placed a few slices of bacon in it. Then she poured a glass of orange juice.

As she placed the jug of juice back in the refrigerator, she recalled how overjoyed she was a few years earlier when, over Thanksgiving dinner, her dad had announced that come spring he was going to have electricity put into the camp as well as a bath-room with a hot-water tank.

Today, as she cracked two brown eggs into the frying pan, her memories of camp came to the fore. She concentrated on her dad, who personally had created this cottage and, along with her mom, had made it such a welcoming and joy-filled place. Seeing Fred Taylor this morning had reminded her that her dad, probably three or four years older than him, seemed so vastly different. "Strong," "physical," and "kind" were words Chris had formulated in describing her father.

In contrast she thought of Fred Taylor—hospitable, attractive… and egotistical. A strange feeling crept over her about the way he first looked at her today.

She finished her breakfast, cleaned up the dishes, thought momentarily of going for a swim, then decided to read for a bit.

Remember, you don't want to get a cramp. Even without her presence here, Chris could hear her mother's voice distinctly. These were the words her mom had so frequently spoken in Chris's growing-up years and words she still heeded today.

A short time later, when she felt she had waited long enough, she walked out the front door and to the dock. She took a shallow dive into what felt like bathwater. She swam parallel to shore for the length of a football field and back, then walked out of the water and shook herself off. She grabbed a towel she'd left on the front porch. It wasn't that she was rushing, but she needed to clear her head, and there were questions to deal with.

Within a few minutes, out of her wet swimsuit, she climbed into a pair of well-worn blue jeans, a long-sleeve shirt, and hiking boots. Her red daypack was prepared for today's journey, with a can of soda, a cucumber sandwich, a Granny Smith apple, a canteen of water, and some bug spray to add to the survival and first-aid kits she always carried.

A feeling flooded over Chris as she journeyed northeast, one she hadn't experienced lately. She wasn't quite sure how to define it. Was it freedom, being in control, or a feeling of adventure?

What lies ahead for me? she wondered.

Whatever she had been experiencing, this was the first time she had mentally articulated the thoughts. She had spent so much time contemplating the end of her marriage that she had given little heed to which choices were now hers to make as a single woman. She'd have to give this some serious thought during her time at camp.

A half-hour later, full of hope and expectation for the climb ahead of her, she parked at the trailhead of Blue Mountain. This would be her fourth or fifth climb up this stately mountain; she couldn't be sure. Each time she hiked its rugged trail, she noticed the erosion. Areas that once had a firm soil base were now totally bare. Her hiking boots provided ample support for her ankles, and after twenty minutes of climbing, she fell into a steady rhythm.

She made it to the top in less than two hours, enjoying the workout the climb provided. Tired and sweaty she walked to the top of the exposed granite and surveyed a 360-degree view of the earth's lakes and trees that were now in her line of sight. The view from the top didn't disappoint, and she thought that is exactly why one climbs—for the joy of seeing the world below you as the eagle does.

With a bright-August sun illuminating her world, she removed her pack and sat down, as a very pleasant breeze continued to dry her hair. Nearby was the brass surveyor's plate that Verplanck Colvin had placed there. Chris thought it might very well have been a day like today, a hundred years before, when in his survey of the Adirondack Mountains he had climbed this particular one. *Maybe he sat down right here,* she thought. *I just hope his enjoyment was as great as mine. Could this day be any more beautiful?*

She lay back on the bare, cool rocks and stared off into the deep-blue heavens. This was the first time since she had left home, just twenty-four hours ago, that she really missed David and wished he could take all of this in with her. He had understood her need to take time away this week and "get her head on straight." In recent weeks David had mentioned marriage more than once; he hadn't really proposed to her, but he put the suggestion out there. He'd now been a widower for more than a year, and Chris's annulment had been finalized. As Catholics they could marry in the Church at any time. This was very important to Chris. If and when she married again, she wanted to be sure the sacrament of matrimony was conferred in a church.

The biggest issue facing her, and the most troublesome, was the fact that in marrying David she would become an instant mother to a nine-year-old son and seven-year-old daughter.

I'm only thirty four. What about my own children? she asked herself.

Chris still wanted to have a baby. She had tried unsuccessfully for the last nine years but was still optimistic. Her doctor, after reviewing her medical file, had assured her that there didn't appear to be any physical reason why she hadn't conceived. But looking at her track record, she wondered if stepchildren might possibly be the only children she'd ever have. *Will these stepchildren be enough?* she wondered.

The questions lingered, and there still wasn't a ring on her finger.

After her breakup with Mike, she couldn't be sure she'd ever find a man who so measured up to all the qualities she desired in a mate. But David certainly did. There was no doubt, absolutely none, that she would be happy with him. When thinking about his children, Chris often asked herself, *Why is it always so much about what I want? Am I being selfish?*

As she lay on the mountain, she made plans to spend time in meditation this week, praying for the spirit to guide her in her choices. But for the moment, she had a lunch waiting in her pack. She retrieved the food items and placed them on a dishtowel she'd thought to place in the pack. Slowly and deliberately she ate the victuals and savored the flavors that crossed her lips.

She recalled a climb up this mountain during her and Mike's first year of marriage when she had secretly packed a bottle of Champagne in her pack. Upon reaching the summit, they relished their feelings of exhilaration, the view, and the opportunity to enjoy the small lunch she had brought. When Chris took the bottle of Champagne out of her pack, Mike burst out in laughter.

"You're something else, Chris," Mike told her. "Here. Let me pop the cork."

As the cork emerged, the contents bubbled up and over the top. Now they were both laughing, which continued as Chris drew two tin cups from her pack.

"It isn't Waterford crystal, but I'm sure the Champagne will taste just as good." She couldn't remember in her life a more interesting spot for her to enjoy her favorite drink.

Today there was no Champagne at the top of Blue Mountain, but the water in her canteen was refreshing and did, in fact, hit the spot.

When she was ready to head down, she didn't look back for one last panoramic view, which wasn't unusual. She already had captured the picture-postcard scene. She wanted to get down and off the mountain. True to form, she set her feet in motion and, lickety-split, in a few minutes was well below the summit. She slowed for some oncoming hikers, but as usual they conceded to her as they would anyone heading down the mountain. She thought of the upcoming choices she had to make in the very near future.

She descended quickly and arrived back at her car in about half the time as her ascent. *That was moving*, she thought, but her calves were throbbing. *Oh, the price we pay!*

She slipped out of her hiking boots and into a pair of flip-flops she'd put in the car earlier, which provided cool comfort to her hot, sweaty feet. Working out the cramps, she walked up and down the parking area. It gave her time to think, and quite spontaneously she decided to find a telephone in the village of Blue Mountain Lake so she could call David. Hopefully he'd be at his desk working on an article.

After driving the mile down Route 30 into the hamlet of Blue Mountain Lake, she found a phone booth and some change she had tucked away in her glove compartment. She dropped a quarter into the slot, dialed his number, and heard the operator interrupt to say, "That will be fifty-five cents for the first three minutes." She dropped the additional coins in and heard David pick up the phone on the first ring. In his voice she heard the delight he felt at her call. They chatted about the day's events and closed in her allotted time with an "I love you."

After the call she returned to the highway, where Route 28 intersected with Route 30, heading southwest back to camp along the familiar route. As she slowed along Raquette Lake, where a full and perfect view of Blue Mountain was possible, she was absolutely sure the person who'd had the naming rights had gotten it right. Especially on this day—off in the distance—blue it was.

When she opened the back door of the camp, a cool wave of air flooded over her, in contrast to the eighty-degree day she was enjoying. She emptied her pack and before long was standing in a very warm shower, delighting in how delicious it felt on her body. After wrapping her hair in a towel, she donned a pair of Bermudas and a top and walked into the kitchen, where she mixed herself a gin and tonic and squeezed a wedge of lime.

Gosh, I feel good, was all Chris could think. *It's my first full day, and I've already gotten in a canoe ride, gone swimming, and climbed up Blue, and now I have a gin and tonic in hand. Is it any wonder I love camp so much?*

She quickly cleared out her daypack, making it clean and ready for the next hike. She slipped into her flip-flops and headed for the dock; on her way she picked up her spiral notebook and ballpoint pen. She'd been working on a bicentennial piece for a regional magazine, and her deadline was approaching. As she often did, she felt she could mix a little work time with pleasure.

Relaxing in an Adirondack chair, she gazed out at her surroundings, noting how different the sky appeared than it had nine hours earlier. Huge cumulous clouds hung on the horizon, casting dark shadows on the mountains. The sun continued to beat down with intensity, but a delightful lake breeze kept her comfortable. When she had climbed out of the shower, she was surprised to note her body already had picked up some tan.

Chris reflected on her earlier phone call to David, the sound of his voice, confident and reassuring, and her earlier thoughts about whether marriage between them was viable. She laid down her notebook on the arm of the chair, closed her eyes, and immersed herself in prayer. She reviewed all the information she had mulled over concerning marriage to David. Suddenly she realized, *You've responded "yes" to all the questions, Chris. So what's the problem?*

She stayed with the question. She loved thinking about being married to David and what the years ahead might hold in store for them. Being alone this week, she knew she had plenty of time to consider those possibilities. She was hopeful that David's eagerness, and his pressure, wouldn't become the deciding factors. She was feeling strange and independent. It was the 1970s. The world had changed. A woman could make her own choices.

She prayed. She wrote. Several hours later, the article she had been writing now complete, she decided on a light dinner—a garden salad and fresh fruit—and a little reading before lights out. Around eight she crawled into bed and read a few chapters of James Michener's *Centennial*, her camp novel for the summer. Before it was dark, she fell into a deep slumber.

CHAPTER 8

As Chris glanced at the round, metal alarm clock on the dresser, there was just enough light for her to see the dial and realize it was six-thirty. As she raised the white shade, she saw a bright and sunny morning. She dressed quickly and, once on the front porch, was grateful she'd added a sweatshirt to her outfit, as the thermometer mounted on a porch post read fifty-eight. She recalled how extreme the range in temperatures could be in August between daytime highs and nighttime lows.

Once she was on the lake, it felt much warmer, and before long she lay down her paddle to pull off her sweatshirt, unsure whether it was the sun, the exercise, or a combination of both.

Another gorgeous day, she thought. The lake was like a mirror, and reflections from the surrounding landscape met the water in such an unbroken manner that it was difficult to visually figure out where reality left off and its reflection began.

She rounded the elongated island at the far end of the lake and headed for home. It was quiet; even the loons were silent, though, keeping a watchful eye, Chris caught sight of them at a distance. The pair swam apart, making frequent dives far beneath the surface in pursuit of their breakfast. Many times in the past, she had stopped to watch these beautiful endangered birds. Having a pair nest on this lake year after year made the lake even more special.

Depending on the pacing of her paddling and with what strength and vigor she decided to pull with, on average she could make the round trip in about an hour. Of course it all depended on her curiosity on any given morning. Was there something along the shoreline that was calling for her to check out—an unusual flowering plant, a fungus, or a gnarly root?

Only ten minutes from her camp, she suddenly caught the image of Fred Taylor waving her down from the end of his dock. He stood in dungarees and a green flannel shirt, coffee mug in hand.

"I've got your coffee ready for you," he hollered.

Chris yelled back, "Good morning." Momentarily she thought to shout out, "Sorry, I've got to get back to camp." Then she thought, *He's gone to all this trouble. What's the harm? Shouldn't I pull over to his dock and accept his offer of morning coffee?*

When she had paddled by a half-hour earlier, she hadn't seen a sign of anyone. Now there he stood, with a stance and demeanor that reminded her of Carl—casual, inviting, pleasant, and with a welcoming grin. Perhaps he wanted to make amends. Fred Taylor was a figure from her past. David was her future. Wasn't it time to move on?

"It's just a cup of coffee," Chris murmured. As she pulled the canoe alongside the dock, Fred knelt, eager to assist her.

As she stepped onto the dock with Fred's help, she had the distinct feeling that he had held her hand a bit too long. She took the mug he offered and voiced her thank-you as they both settled into the deck chairs. Fred immediately wanted to know what she had been up to, and Chris shared, in very descriptive terms, her climb up Blue Mountain the day before.

"It was an absolutely beautiful day, and lots of hikers were on the trail. I really enjoyed it," Chris said, her hands expressing her enthusiasm.

From her descriptions and knowledge of the trail, Fred inquired, "When did you become so passionate about hiking and mountain climbing?"

His questions became the perfect opportunity for Chris to talk about her years as a coed, when she had joined a hiking group at college.

"When I was a teenager, my family did some hiking and climbing here in the Adirondacks, but it wasn't until I met a professor at school that I got hooked on serious hiking and survival education. On Saturdays he'd make arrangements to drive a college station wagon and take five or six of us to hike trails in the nearby Catskill Mountains. It was great exercise and so exhilarating. I fell in love with hiking after my first outing with the group. And I still love it."

When Chris finished her tale, she sensed that she had been dominating the conversation, so she quickly turned toward Fred and offered, "I remember Carl telling me you have a great love of music. He said you not only teach it but you also play a couple of instruments."

"You remembered correctly," Fred said, his eyes lighting up. "I'm still teaching music in the city schools of Cortland, and I still play the saxophone pretty seriously."

Over the next ten minutes, Fred talked about his teaching career and shared that he had formed a jazz combo in the early sixties that was known as The Blue Notes. "I brought my sax along with me here so I can practice and also work on a couple of new arrangements for the group," he said.

Chris wanted to know more. "Where do you play? Does Carl ever get to hear you?"

"It's funny that you ask that. My combo played at Carl's wedding reception. I had a substitute replace me for the day, but I did play 'Everybody Loves Somebody Sometime'—you know, the Dean Martin hit—for their first dance together. The group plays at weddings and other types of parties, but lately we've been playing on a lot of college campuses in Central New York. Is there anything else you'd like to know about me?"

"No, I guess that covers it." Chris didn't want to feed his ego, and yet Fred's air of self-confidence strangely intrigued her.

Her memory of Carl, by contrast, was how carefree he was, never taking himself too seriously. She wondered, *But that was when he was a teenager. Did he grow up to be like his father?*

They both sat in silence for a short while, until Fred, perhaps sensing it was uncomfortable, asked Chris, "Any mountains to climb today?"

"No, I promised my mom I'd clean the camp. We usually do this together sometime in August, but since I knew I'd have the time, I thought I'd offer so they can enjoy the fruits of my labor when they spend next week here. And frankly I enjoy doing it."

"After all that work, why don't you drive over here around six, and I'll barbecue some steaks for dinner? I'm all by my lonesome here. You can listen to some of the music I brought along with me."

"I really appreciate your offer," she said, "but are you sure you want to go to all that trouble? After all you're on vacation."

"It's no problem. I'm happy to do it, Chris."

She thought about the evening to come. "Since I'm not that far away, maybe I'll paddle over."

"Are you sure? It may be dark when you leave."

"Oh, not to worry. There's a full moon tonight, and I don't expect it to be overcast if the day continues like it started out."

As Chris rose and placed her mug on the arm of her chair, Fred looked directly at her. He seemed to be very good at making eye contact. Reaching for her elbow, he said, "Great. I look forward to seeing you at six."

As Chris climbed into the canoe and paddled back, a feeling of uneasiness filled her. *What am I getting myself into?* she wondered. The question wouldn't be answered until a dozen hours later.

She wondered whether her acceptance of dinner was the right idea. Was it the memories of Carl that she wanted to revisit? Was being with his father a chance for her to think about Carl in happier times?

Whatever her reasoning, she had made the decision. She felt the die had been cast, as it were, and there was no practical way for her to renege on Fred's invitation. She decided to make the best of it.

Returning to Lake Wrights, Chris started in on her cleaning project after a quick breakfast. After climbing the stairs to the loft, she cleaned the two bedrooms on the second floor, where she washed windows, dusted, swept floors, and shook out rugs. The beds were still nicely made from their most recent use, with quilts folded at the foot end of each, awaiting their next use.

As often as she and her mother had cleaned the camp, Chris always looked upon the act as therapeutic. Why she felt this way, she couldn't be sure. But when a house, or in this case Lake Wrights, was clean and tidy, dusted and set aright, she also felt clean and fresh. There was something about the order of things, everything being in its place. No one ever appreciated the hard work and energy expended in making her apartment or the camp look immaculate—that is, except her mother.

She recalled summer vacations here when, on any given rainy day, Mrs. Wright, while setting out breakfast for her children, would say, "What do you think? Should we attack the attic today and really give it a going over?"

What fun we had as kids, Chris recalled, thinking how cleverly her mother had transformed work into play.

She held on to that thought as she continued her work on the main floor. She dusted bookshelves, lamps, and furniture. She wiped off the mantle, washed the antique kerosene lamps, including their chimneys, and wiped down the walls. When the floors were done, she washed the windows and curtains as well.

With the sun this bright, they'll be dry in no time, she thought, as she hung them out to dry. *I'll re-hang them before I leave for dinner.*

She took a quick break at noon for a tuna fish sandwich and a glass of milk, and then it was back to the housecleaning. She noted that she was making headway. Things that had gone unnoticed now sparkled, and she was pleased with her progress. Her mother would be happy. Saving the kitchen for last, she discovered more to clean than she had envisioned and didn't finish her project until almost five o'clock.

Before her shower she made a quick trip upstairs to collect a dust mop and dust rags she'd left there. Everything she'd used to clean the camp was now stored away until the next time they'd be needed, and she ran outside to check on the curtains. As she had hoped, they were dry. She carried them indoors over her arm and quickly re-hung them. Standing back to take an admiring look, she thought, *They look so clean. When was the last time anyone washed them? I hope you'll be pleased, Mom.* But then could anyone ever do a job as perfectly as her mother could?

As she turned to walk down the hall, she felt happy about all the energy and effort she had expended today. In the bathroom she dropped out of her dirty shorts and top; she already could feel the shower. She delighted in the steamy droplets as they hit her tired body. She was used to quick four-to-five-minute showers, but today she lingered and spent a few additional minutes letting the shower beat down on her back. It felt so refreshing.

She dried off, rubbed the towel briskly over her hair, and was thankful for her hairdryer and hot rollers. With her hair up in curlers, she picked up her mess of clothes and headed for her bedroom, where she decided to wear a blue cotton pantsuit embellished with Native American beading. Then she slipped on a pair of brown sandals.

It was closing in on five-thirty when she emerged from the bedroom, her hair beautifully coiffed. It was the first time since her arrival that she really had primped herself.

Why are you fussing? she thought. *This isn't a date.*

She thought it would be nice to bring along a bottle of wine for dinner, but there was none to be had. There was beer in the refrigerator and liquor in the cupboard but no wine.

Usually at this time of the day, she'd have fixed herself a bourbon Manhattan, but unsure of what Fred might offer, she thought the wiser of it. The clock read five forty.

I've got to get going, she told herself. Not knowing how cool it would be upon her return, she grabbed a sweatshirt and headed out the front door.

The lake was calm as she maneuvered the canoe slowly, so as not to drip water from the paddle on to her outfit. She also didn't want to work up a sweat.

Ten minutes later she pulled alongside the dock, where she spotted Fred in front of a barbecue grill, flames leaping into the air. Chris stepped onto the dock then bent down to grab the rope and secure it. She walked slowly to where Fred now seemed to have the charcoal under control.

"Good evening, Chris. How beautiful you look. This'll take a while before it's ready for the steaks. How about a drink? All I can offer is scotch and water. Will that do?"

"That sounds fine to me," she said.

Scotch wasn't a liquor Chris drank very often, but she remembered that the girls from her sorority house in college, on occasion, would go to their favorite watering hole and all order scotch and soda. Then they'd stand around, arm in arm, singing, "Scotch and soda, mud in your eye... Baby, do I feel high... Oh, me... Oh, my... Boy, do I feel high!"

Chris had settled into a chair on the lawn near the barbecue grill. A few moments later, Fred returned with two highball glasses. As he approached her, she detected the scent of Irish Spring. She noted that, in anticipation of her arrival, he had showered and shaved off his two- or three-day growth of beard and had dressed in a pair of khaki pants and a green T-shirt with LIFE IS BETTER WITH A LITTLE SAX printed across the front.

Interesting play on words, she mused, but she felt uneasy as she thought of his displaying it in front of her. *How insensitive,* she thought, and repressed what she wanted to say, which was, *I'll bet your wife doesn't let you wear that out in public.*

Chris thought again about how much Fred physically reminded her of Carl. *I can't believe Carl would ever behave like this. If only it was the old days and that was Carl standing there,* she thought wistfully.

Lifting her glass, she said, "Cheers."

Fred sat down opposite her; both chairs were positioned at an angle that offered a magnificent view of the lake. She was grateful he wasn't facing her directly, so she could avoid having to look at his shirt.

"What a gorgeous night to cook out," she said. "Thank you again for the invitation. I don't think I had enough energy left to prepare dinner tonight."

"Glad to be of service, Chris. How did your housecleaning go?" he asked, slapping a mosquito that had alit on his forearm.

"I couldn't be happier. It went very well. I'm sure my folks will be pleased, and that's all that matters. Oh, by the way, I should have brought a bottle of wine for dinner but didn't realize we didn't have any at camp. When I finished cleaning, it was too late to run into Inlet to buy one."

"That's all right. When I went into town to get the steaks, I picked up a bottle of Burgundy. I hope you like that."

"It's my favorite, especially with a good steak." Chris thought of how much alcohol she might consume over the next hour or two and made a mental note to watch it. "And how did your day go?" she asked Fred. "Any luck working on those new charts?"

For the next ten minutes, Fred shared in great detail his work throughout the day; he had looked over sheet music and transcribed it for sax, piano, drums, and bass.

"I'm pretty good at it," he said. "It takes time, but some of the arrangements I've put together sound great. The group loves playing new stuff, and no one else in the group has the time or inclination to do it, although they're always offering me suggestions."

"I'm surprised you could get away for vacation these two weeks without it interfering with engagements," Chris offered, having settled back in her chair and crossed her legs.

"All the guys in the combo except one are teachers, so we always reserve these middle two weeks of August for everyone's vacation time. It works well. Everyone gets back from vacation relaxed, renewed, and ready to start the school year."

A half-hour passed without Chris realizing she had consumed her drink as if it were water. She was feeling mellow.

I should have had more water to drink after I cleaned, she thought, realizing she was probably a bit dehydrated. Fred excused himself to retrieve the steaks and grabbed Chris's empty glass on the way.

"Let me get you another. It seems to be going down well."

Chris thought again that she should limit what she was drinking, but the scotch and soda appeared not to be too strong, so she thought, *What'll be the harm with just one more?*

Then, remembering she had to get herself and the canoe back home after dinner, she called out, "Go easy on the scotch."

Minutes later she sipped on the refreshed drink ever so slowly and watched as Fred barbecued two nice-looking rib eyes. She felt relaxed and enjoyed the sound of the sizzle of raw meat as it cooked on the grill. She breathed in deeply the aromas floating by.

It felt good that she could be herself, let her hair down, and not worry about a thing. Someone else was in charge, for the moment, cooking dinner and serving up the drinks. It seemed right that she could simply sit back and enjoy it.

As Fred stood at the grill, Chris continued to wish Carl were standing there instead. Even so, for a man in his fifties, Fred had a fantastic physique. He filled out the T-shirt nicely.

Tongs in hand, he turned to Chris and declared, "I make a mean marinade, and the meat has been bathing in it all afternoon."

There he goes again, Chris thought, then offered, "Is there anything I can do to help?"

"I've got it covered. We'll eat inside. I thought that would be a bit easier."

Steaks cooked, Fred led Chris into the small camp. He set the platter on a round wooden table that had plastic place mats and paper napkins topped with mismatched plates.

The interior of the cabin appeared quite utilitarian. A tan, wood paneling covered the walls of the one main front room that served as a combination living and dining room. The out-of-date furnishings were modest. The Adirondack-themed furniture showed wear but other-wise appeared neat and clean. Fred's saxophone stood in its stand, off to one side of the seating area. And next to it a music stand stood in front of an upright chair and music sheets were neatly stacked nearby.

Fred walked over to a cassette player and turned it on. He returned to the table, where he filled small juice glasses with the red wine. He sat down opposite Chris as she began to recognize the Dave Brubeck Quartet and Paul Desmond on the saxophone.

Glancing down at the table, Fred said apologetically, "When you rent a camp, there aren't a lot of choices. You have to do with what you've got."

Chris knew all about that. A lot of hand-me-downs were at her camp, along with many not-so-up-to-date items. Wineglasses had yet to make their way to Lake Wrights also.

The smell of the grilled steaks made Chris realize how hungry she was. Her stomach had been growling for the last half-hour. A small ceramic bowl of potato salad sat on the table as well as a wooden bowl full of chef salad. Chris usually would have said grace before eating, but she'd learned, when she was growing up, that "when in Rome do as the Romans do." So she said the words, "Bless us, O Lord, and these thy gifts, which we are about to receive from thy bounty through Christ our Lord. Amen" quietly to herself.

After her first few bites, she declared, "This steak is excellent."

"When I do the cooking, you not only get the steak but the sizzle as well."

The music drifted through the camp, and Chris and Fred made small talk. Glancing over at her he said, "I should have lit some candles and made it a perfectly romantic evening."

Chris didn't know how to respond to Fred's words as they swirled through her head. She couldn't be sure when she had stopped thinking of Carl. Her eyes met Fred's, and she smiled. She had to acknowledge that she was attracted to the man who sat across the table from her and had to admit, even without candles, that this was a very romantic setting.

Was this the alcohol speaking?

Halfway through the meal, Chris grew uncomfortable about how the evening was unfolding. The conversation was going along smoothly, but she was analyzing Fred's sharing, subtleties, and innuendos. As a writer she was all too familiar with the unwritten word, implication, and inference.

I'm rather naive not to recognize what's being played out here—two attractive people, one small room, good food, alcohol, music. Fred has certainly set the stage. I just need to learn my lines.

As the tape continued, Fred said, "I love this music and think it's a classic jazz recording."

With "Take Five" now filling the camp with sound, Chris asked, "Fred, do you play your saxophone like that?"

He responded, "That number is in the combo's repertoire, and I do give it my best." As he continued to talk about his group, he periodically interrupted with, "Listen to this passage."

He rose to pour more wine in her glass and placed his left hand on her shoulder. She was momentarily startled. Suddenly she thought, *You're the one who's put yourself in this predicament.*

She wanted to think this was all innocent on the surface—the father of an old boyfriend taking pity on her after a day of housework and making her dinner. But right now she couldn't remember another life experience where she had placed herself in such a compromising situation.

She asked herself, *How do I get myself out of this?*

Her concerns focused on David and what he would think right now if he saw her.

Calm down, Chris, she told herself. *Perhaps you're overreacting.*

Fred sat back down and asked Chris how she was enjoying her steak.

"This food is far superior to anything I could have whipped up at camp tonight. Thank you for taking pity on me and inviting me to dinner. I appreciate it," Chris shared in good humor.

Fred raised his full glass of wine and offered, "Here's to Chris Wright, who I once knew as a teenager and now is single once more."

Chris raised her glass, unsure where Fred had conceived of the words in his toast. *What was that supposed to mean?*

Almost finished with her food, she glanced around the room, looking for anything that might prompt a question or change the flow of conversation. She didn't want Fred's present train of thought to continue.

"I see the camp owner has provided you with a couple of kerosene lamps," she said." They're always handy to have when the power goes out."

"Hopefully I won't need to use them over these two weeks, unless we have a bad thunder and lightning storm. Do you still use them at your camp, or do you have electricity now?" Fred asked. "I remember Carl always talking about the big glass kerosene lamps you had burning in your camp back when he met you."

Chris felt better at this point; the focus was on her camp and Carl.

"We do have electricity now. My dad had it installed three or four years ago, and what a difference it's made. We still use those kerosene lamps, though. It seems that two or three times a summer there's a storm or an accident, and we usually lose power during thunderstorms. Power poles snap, or trees and limbs fall on power lines. Most of the time, power is restored within a few hours, but in the meantime, we have enough light from the lamps to read or play cards by. It's always my dad's excuse to go to bed early."

"Not a bad idea," Fred interjected.

Chris, regretting what she'd just said, continued, "It's unbelievable sometimes for me to think of all the years before we had electricity. We'd cook on a kerosene stove and use the outhouse and not think a thing about it. It was camp!"

As Chris finished her little talk, Fred offered coffee as he picked up the plates and took them, she assumed, to the kitchen, which she couldn't see from where she sat. He returned with two mugs of coffee, having prepared Chris's with sugar and milk. He emptied what was left of the wine in their glasses.

"I need to finish up this coffee and wine and be on my way soon," Chris voiced strongly. She had made a decision and wanted to be on record as being opposed to any ulterior motives Fred might be contemplating.

"It's still early," he responded.

Under any other circumstances, she thought, this would be a perfect evening. She felt euphoric after her productive day of cleaning, the excellent dinner, and the spirits. There were times like this when she felt childlike, when all things seemed to come together in such loveliness and harmony, making for a perfect evening; even the background music was superb.

But right now she was feeling the effects of the alcohol. She had sensed it earlier when she began to ramble on about everything over dinner; it was a sure sign to her that she was a bit tipsy.

She was aware that the sun had set; the camp grew dim as daylight faded.

"In the old days, this is when we'd light our kerosene lamps," Chris shared. "Do you think we need some light?"

"I can still see your lovely eyes, and that's all that matters," Fred responded. "Do you mind if I light up my pipe?"

When Chris responded, "Not at all," he filled his pipe from a tobacco pouch and lit it. The room filled with the smoke, carrying with it its pleasant and fragrant odor. Now, however, not only was the smoke getting in her eyes, but it also was going to her head. She knew that if she was going to make a move for departure, it had to be soon.

She stood up and, looking down, said, "Fred, thank you so much for the great meal and evening, but I'd best be going."

He stood and moved in front of Chris, reaching for her hand. He took it in his, raised it slowly to his lips, and kissed it. "You know I don't deserve your kindness, Chris. I don't know how you've been able to get over how mean I was to you once. I'm sure glad you could overlook our rough start so many years ago and turn this into one memorable week for me."

What is he talking about? Chris thought. *My kindness? Overlook his meanness? Didn't I tell him I'd forgive but not forget? And what memorable week is he talking about?*

He held on to her hand. His was warm and supple. He continued to stare into her eyes. Chris, although unprepared, seemed to know exactly the direction Fred was headed—and she wasn't resisting his advances. He took her into his arms, saying nothing but simply holding her in a tight embrace. She was barefoot, realizing that sometime between entering the camp and this moment she had slipped off her sandals. He held her close, and the odors from the barbecue filled her nostrils. He was warm, and his body heat radiated through his shirt. Her head rested in the comfortable hollow between his neck and shoulder, a position she loved to experience with David. Here, she and Fred simply stood, locked in an embrace.

She felt it was wrong, but she wasn't fighting the hold Fred had on her. What to do? She pushed away, or at least tried to, but Fred kept a strong grip on her.

Finally she spoke up, "Really, Fred. I've got to go. I can't stay here."

"Why not? You're not married anymore."

"But *you* are!" Chris affirmed.

"I have a very understanding wife," Fred responded.

Chris could feel his warmth, his pounding heart. She smelled the lingering tobacco on his breath as he repositioned her body and looked directly into her eyes. His lips met hers softly and gently. Then the kiss became more intense, and his tongue forced apart her lips.

Chris withdrew and tried to pull away from his grasp but couldn't overpower him. He kissed her again, and all she could think was, *If this has to be happening, why isn't it with Carl?*

Fred continued to kiss her, and she felt his manhood press against her body. Holding on to her with one arm, he unsnapped her top with the other.

"Please, Fred. Don't do this," she said.

But he wasn't listening. Chris realized she was now succumbing to his advances, as her womanhood was tingling. She lingered in the kiss, and a passion stirred within her that she hadn't expected. She loved the feeling. She didn't want him to stop.

She seemed to be looking down on this scene from afar, perhaps wishing to be the observer rather than the participant. Everything took place in slow motion.

Fred's hands gently caressed her body, growing stronger as he now groped her breasts. Her top and bra fell to the floor, and his mouth now reached her orbs, which he sucked on, right to left. He picked her up and carried her down a dark hallway and into a bedroom. He laid her on a bed that was already open to the sheets.

Oh, my God, Chris thought. *He planned this from the start.*

Quickly he grabbed her garments at the waist and in one yank pulled them off her body. He was out of his clothes in seconds and immediately dropped down on top of her.

Please let this be over quickly, Chris prayed.

CHAPTER 9

Three hours later, as she sat on the edge of her bed, Chris's head swirled with conflicting emotions over what had just happened.

What an animal. How did I let myself get roped into all his sweet-talking? Perhaps if she thought the worst of Fred, she could place all the blame on him.

Wrapped up in her bathrobe, she towel-dried her hair. *What did I do to cause this?* She came to the realization that she had played a part in the recent sexual escapade.

She lay back on her bed pillows, leaving the light on, and stared off into space, reflecting on what had transpired. She couldn't be sure of the sequence of events; her head was still swimming from the alcohol she had consumed. Before she had showered, feeling nauseous, she had vomited. Although she felt relieved of her physical discomfort, her head spun with feelings of disgust.

What she did remember was that Fred had had his way with her. He had caressed and probed her body, quickly and harshly. He had explored her from head to toe, never asking her what she might desire. Fred was in his own world, one of control. She felt man-handled. She remembered the sensation as he kissed her inner thighs, his hands as they grasped her buttocks, his tongue on her nipples. Only one other man had made love to her in her entire life, Mike, and she never had experienced such a prolonged physical assault as Fred had given her body. She remembered the tobacco taste inside her mouth and how she could smell it in her hair as she lay in his bed. He hadn't climaxed quickly and lingered as she languished. He never asked her, through it all, how she was feeling.

She remembered lying there for what seemed forever. When she heard him drift off to sleep and begin to snore, she slipped out of bed and found her pants and panties on the floor. Remembering the route Fred had taken to the bedroom, and grateful for the full moon, she retraced his steps as silently as possible and found her way back to the living room.

There was enough light shining through the windows for her to easily find her bra and top. She redressed and found her sandals by the front door.

As she moved quietly out the screen door and off the porch, the full moon provided ample light for her to see her tethered canoe. She untied the rope and paddled away.

It was as if she was momentarily transported to another time and place when she softly murmured aloud, "What a gorgeous moonlit night this is. I don't ever remember being alone on Seventh Lake at this hour."

She felt like she was in a different world, not one with riddled memories of the past few hours. Perhaps it was her way of trying to block out the reality of what had occurred and instead dwell on the beauty of her surroundings.

In years to come, this will be the remembrance I have of my time at camp, Chris now determined, as she pulled up to her own dock.

She walked back up the path to camp, everything in her view awash in moon glow. Her mood of denial was shattered as her sandal hit the first step onto the porch.

On such a night as this, how could a man who's old enough to be my father so abuse me? she asked herself.

Didn't you love it, Chris? When was the last time Mike made love to you like this?

She stood for a moment, leaning on the newel post. *I knew there was a reason I'd hated him,* she thought, then countered with, *As rough as the sex was, wasn't there an excitement about it?*

Returning to the reality of the moment, Chris stared at the crucifix on the wall opposite her bed and thought, *Dear God, what must you be thinking of me? I knew I shouldn't have had that much to drink. Oh, I am so sorry.*

When Chris had reentered camp, she felt dirty and violated and only hoped that a hot shower and vigorously brushing her teeth would remove any evidence of her encounter with Fred Taylor.

Really, Chris? she thought. *If the opportunity presented itself again, wouldn't you agree to it?*

Whatever her feelings, she knew that the memory and the emotions she felt as a result of her experience would be with her for some time to come.

She glanced at her clothes, all in a pile on the floor, where she had left them. She wondered if or when she might wear them again after laundering them.

Why not, Chris? It's a powerful reminder.

She removed the towel from her hair, ran a comb through her damp locks, put on a summer nightgown, and went to bed. Out of exhaustion or the amount of alcohol she had consumed, she was asleep in minutes. Maybe she could sleep off what had happened and never think of it again—sweet dreams that would counteract her present anxiety.

Moonlight cascaded into her room as she opened her eyes. She could make out the dial on the alarm clock that stood on her nightstand—two thirty.

I've only been asleep for three hours? she thought in disbelief.

She flipped on the lamp, put on her robe, grabbed her novel, and headed into the living room. She was about to curl up in one of the overstuffed rockers and attempt to read but felt called to the loft. Seeking support from the cedar handrail, she walked up the staircase. At the top she flipped on the overhead light then walked to the far bedroom, where an old double brass bed stood under the large curtained window.

She piled the pillows against the bedstead and, after pulling the patchwork quilt up from the bottom of the bed, opened her novel. She wouldn't remember how long she had read or when the warmth of Grandma Wright's quilt had supplied enough comfort for her to drop the book and fall fast asleep.

When she awoke she had no idea what time it was. She felt, in so many ways, like a child again, waking up under this quilt in a fetal position, curled up and feeling snuggly. The room was bright with the morning sunshine, and streams of light shone directly on the bed. It took her a while to understand why she was waking up in the loft. Then snapshots of the evening before appeared in her head. She stretched her five-foot-five frame out as far as she could and raised herself up in bed.

Was I hoping to recapture those innocent days of my youth, many of them spent right here?

She straightened the pillows, placed them back under the spread, and refolded the patchwork quilt. As she started down the stairs, she flipped off the light switch, only now realizing the lights had been on all night.

As she walked across the main floor, she surveyed the immaculate kitchen. *You did a good job, Chris,* she proudly thought. When she had left to go to dinner the evening before, everything was clean and neat, and that's what greeted her now.

I left the place immaculate, and I returned to it not so, she confessed, as she recalled Fred roughly disrobing her. *Why was I so totally unprepared for what happened last night?*

If her mother had talked to her more honestly during her growing-up years, maybe this situation might never have presented itself. She would have been on high alert.

He forced me to have sex with him, she thought. *On the other hand, wasn't I the willing partner?* She found herself wrestling within herself, her thoughts and feelings battling with one another.

She glanced at the kitchen clock, noting that 8:00 a.m. was a bit late for her morning canoe trip. Usually by now the lake would start kicking up and "canoe-ready water" would be a has-been. She thought about a possible late-afternoon paddle when the lake would calm down again and she wouldn't have to fight the waves and current. She also decided that on any and all canoe trips for the rest of the week she would paddle directly out from the dock, across the lake, and into Sixth Lake, where she would be far removed from the eyesight of Fred Taylor.

I never want to see him again, she thought. *I wonder what he thought when he woke up this morning and I wasn't in bed with him?*

She gave thought to the fact that he might not want to see her again either. At his camp she hadn't seen a canoe, only a rowboat, and she couldn't be sure whether, remembering where Lake Wrights was located, he might row down the lake to see her.

She made some coffee and put the pot on the gas burner. After getting dressed, she brushed her straight hair back into a ponytail and walked out and up the driveway quickly.

As she climbed the hill that led to the highway, she remembered that many camp owners in the late sixties had named their camps. Her dad had created a sign with LAKE WRIGHTS painted on it and hung it from a post alongside the driveway. It was so helpful in assisting visitors as they tried to locate the entrance to their camp. The rest of the lodges also were built near the lake and were a sizable distance from the heavily wooded Route 28. The sign could be removed from its hooks each fall then taken home and repainted for the next season.

Chris reached for the sign, unhooked it, and carried it back down the driveway. *If he doesn't know where I am,* she thought, *he can't find me. If he does drive by, I think he'd be too confused to know where I'm located. At least I can hope. Better safe than sorry.*

She didn't know whether this action was for her protection or simply to make her feel better—less guilty and remorseful.

Will I ever see him again? she wondered.

On her walk back down the driveway, she caught the unmistakable scent of the damp Adirondack earth and took a deep breath. She never tired of it.

She quickened her pace, grateful that she would be back inside momentarily. The mosquitoes were feasting on her ankles. She hadn't thought to apply bug repellent for the short trip.

As she neared the back deck, she gave thought to leaving the camp entirely and returning home. But quickly she resolved to stay. She had planned this vacation, and nothing would interrupt it. Camp was a retreat, safe, and she felt protected here.

The coffee had just started to percolate, and she smelled its aroma as she walked in through the back door. When it was ready, she poured herself a cupful and filled a bowl with corn flakes, then poured herself a glass of orange juice. Sitting at the small kitchen table, she wished she had the morning paper to read. That thought gave her the idea for a drive, after breakfast, into Inlet to buy one. Besides, there was a phone booth near the grocery store, and she could give David a call.

Newspaper tucked under her arm, she put the necessary coins in the slot, and soon the phone was ringing. When David answered, Chris said, "Good morning."

"Hi, Chris. It's good to hear from you. I missed your voice yesterday."

She went on in long detail, explaining her housecleaning the day before. She added more coins when the operator warned that her three minutes were almost up.

"I spent the day cleaning the camp, David, and didn't finish up until late. I didn't get a chance to drive into town. Sorry," she said apologetically.

"I really miss you. Think about coming home early."

"I miss you too, David. You have no idea how much. But I think I need to take this time—kind of like going on a retreat—to really clear my head. I know you understand."

"I do, Chris. I know it was Father Jim's recommendation for you when the annulment came through. Anything he might suggest for either of us as we move forward in our relationship can't be wrong."

"Thanks for understanding," Chris said. "I love you."

"I love you too. Call me tomorrow."

"I'll try. Bye for now."

The call completed, Chris decided to take a quick walk up and down the main street of Inlet, enjoying the many visitors who walked along the sidewalk gawking at the shops; some were headed into the grocery, the hardware store, or one of the many gift and souvenir shops.

After what occurred last night, I was pretty blasé in my conversation with David, she thought. *I do still love him, don't I? Nothing has changed after last night, has it?*

On her drive back to camp, she reflected on her comments to David about the day before. It wasn't as if she had lied, but it certainly wasn't full disclosure. She wondered whether there was any reason for her to ever share with him what had transpired. Probably not.

I'll go to confession and hopefully get rid of it, at least the sinful part, she thought. *I mean, I'm not the one who instigated this.*

Back at Lake Wrights, she sat down in an overstuffed chair and, for the next two hours, devoured the paper. As she sat she realized how uncomfortable she felt and thought, *I can't remember when my insides hurt this much.*

Last night was the first time anyone had been inside her body since she and Mike had made love for the last time. *Has it really been two years?* she wondered. She recognized that the exception was the Pap smear her gynecologist performed annually. *But that never hurt,* she noted.

She returned to her reading after repositioning her body. Newspapers were her business, her love, and her livelihood. She derived so much pleasure from the printed page—whether it was local, national, or world news—to say nothing of the joy she received from doing the daily crossword puzzle. She had read the comics page from the age of six and had clipped most of the recipes she used regularly from a weekly food section. She knew a newspaper inside and out and appreciated having the time to linger over the regular opinion-page columnists.

She recalled a recent article by a columnist expounding on date rape. She had read it at the time but paid no heed to the illuminating details the writer had described. Thinking back on it now, she wondered if perhaps this is what had happened last night.

I was given alcohol and forced into having sex, she thought, but once again she countered herself. *Didn't I agree to go to Fred's camp, drink his alcohol, and linger in his embrace? If that isn't a positive response to his advances, what is? I'm the guilty one here. I enticed Fred. I set up the situation by showing up for dinner. I could have said no to his invitation, and none of this would have happened.*

She could have said no to the scotch and wine and perhaps not been as friendly, encouraging, or complimentary about his cooking.

Was I setting up the perfect situation for all this to happen? Even my enjoyment of the jazz he was playing? If I had wanted it to end, I probably could have done something to prevent his taking advantage of me. Was I the manipulator? Did I set a trap that he fell into? Why didn't I scream?

She sat and rephrased every one of the questions she had formulated. "Was this *my* fault?" she asked herself out loud, but she didn't have any answers.

Let's face it, she thought. *When he threw me down on the bed, I didn't continue to fight. I just lay back and let him have his way with me.*

Her thoughts went to Mike, her first and only sexual partner until now, and she remembered that he always had been so gentle and caring.

Are you being naive, Chris, admitting to your being unschooled when it comes to the art of lovemaking?

She folded up the paper and walked over to the table, where she laid it down. With no forethought she wandered out the front door and into the late-morning sun. She continued to walk to the end of the dock, scaring some preening ducks that jumped back into the water. She stood taking in the glory of the day. The ducks swam by. She loved their presence but hated their droppings, which she would be washing off the dock later. The shouts and laughter of children were audible along the shoreline.

Oh, I think I need to take a hike.

After returning quickly to the camp, she dressed for the trail, threw some food staples into her pack, and was off. It wasn't until she stopped the car before entering the highway that she thought, *Where am I going?* She knew she wanted to hike; she just didn't know where. She sat for a moment then turned left, deciding to drive to Raquette Lake, where she was familiar with a few trails she had navigated in the past.

The fifteen-minute drive was uneventful except for the instant replays that filled Chris's mind. She couldn't shake the images from the previous night—images of Fred's naked body against hers, his hands, his mouth, his penis. And she continued with the repetition of all her unanswered questions.

She was grateful that dinner had been at Fred's rented cottage and that he never had stepped foot in Lake Wrights; he apparently had no need in 1957 to check on his son's activities, and she couldn't be more relieved that in 1976 she hadn't invited him.

If last night had taken place at Lake Wrights, I think I would have died, she thought. *To have had something so evil take place in this sanctuary—I just can't imagine it.* Then she considered her last thoughts. *Am I thinking it was evil because if it had taken place at Lake Wrights I would have sensed the eyes of Mom and Dad on me? Would they have seen me for what I am? Not the sweet, innocent daughter I've always portrayed myself to be?*

Over the years her initial anger toward Fred had abated as the memories of her brief romance with Carl faded. This week she was able to forgive him, only to be betrayed by him.

Betrayed? she thought. *This wasn't a rape, Chris.*

Now her anger grew—at Fred and at herself. No lines seemed to be clear. No right or wrong. No guilty or innocent. She always had prided herself on not hating anyone, a life lesson her parents had taught her. As she had grown into adulthood, she realized she was indifferent to some people she had come to know. She tolerated those she couldn't like, let alone love. She had an acceptance for a lot of human behavior that wasn't to her liking, but in her memory, Fred Taylor had been the only person about whom she had said, "I hate him."

Along with her confessing the sin of fornication, she knew that when she went to confession she'd also have to seek forgiveness for the hatred toward Fred that coursed through her entire being.

Is that what you're feeling, or do you have other feelings that you're trying to hide? she asked herself.

Chris knew that Father Jim always spoke of forgiveness. "If Jesus could forgive those who hung him on a cross, you can forgive too, Chris," he had told her more than once.

She turned left off Route 28, which led to Raquette Lake, a tiny village that sat at the head of yet another beautiful Adirondack lake. Chris remembered repeating stories about the lake her dad had told her; she especially recalled one memorable day when she and Mike had canoed the lake.

"Mike, do you know how the lake got its name?" she had asked.
"I haven't a clue."

"Well, let me tell you. During the Revolutionary War, a group of Tories were heading north through the Adirondacks on snowshoes. Did you know the French word for 'snowshoe' is '*raquette*'? Anyway, apparently there was a spring thaw, and they took off their snowshoes and left them all here in a pile along the shore in seventeen seventy-six. Isn't that fascinating?"

Chris loved this story. It added so much to the lore associated with these mountains, and she remembered Mike being pretty impressed with her history lesson that day.

She continued to drive the short half-mile beyond the village and pulled off the heavily wooded, narrow dirt road and parked.

The trail was all Chris had hoped for, with various topography, hardwoods and pines, streams to navigate, roots and rocks to climb over, birds chirping high above, a blue sky, and lush green undergrowth. She breathed in deeply as she carefully stepped over roots, taking in the smells the forest produced.

Two hours into the hike, she was thrilled that the end of the trail yielded a large open space devoid of anything growing and in which a large fire pit stood in the middle. Several downed logs surrounded the area. Chris sat down on one and took in the spectacular view of the lake.

This is a great place for lunch, she thought. From her daypack she retrieved crackers, an apple, a banana, and a can of soda, all of which she consumed in short order. She unzipped a pocket in the pack and withdrew a prayer book.

After wandering to the water's edge, she placed the little book on a rock, where she took off her boots and socks. Sitting down on the rock with the book now in hand, she dangled her feet into the cold water.

How refreshing, she thought. *But I'll pay for this when I try to put those boots back on.*

She opened the book then leaned against a huge white pine that abutted the rock. She closed her eyes, moved her fanny on the rock to get a bit more comfortable, and soaked in the sun. Whenever Chris hiked alone to a remote location, she felt as if she were the only human on earth—no voices, no noise, just the song of the birds, the wind whistling through the trees, and the lake lapping against the shore. Closing the little book that remained in her lap, she surrendered to her surroundings,.

A half-hour later, she came to an awareness of where she was. She was quite sure she hadn't fallen asleep, but her mind and body certainly had been transported to that place she periodically found in meditation, when she became lost to the world and, as she often said, moved to higher ground.

Slowly, with eyes now wide open and in touch with her surroundings, she drew her feet from the water and pulled on her socks and hiking boots. She set off for the trailhead, motivated to set a little faster pace hiking out, and noted she had cut ten minutes off her time when she reached her car.

When she opened the car door, it felt like an oven inside, and she immediately lowered the windows and left the door open for a little while. After slipping into a pair of flip-flops, and with a breeze now blowing through the vehicle, she turned the car around and headed for camp. As she exited the village, she pulled over in front of St. William's Church and wondered if it might be open on this Wednesday afternoon. She'd give it a try. The door was unlocked, so she entered the old white wooden structure.

Such a simple country church, she thought.

She walked down the aisle and moved into a pew on the right that was halfway to the altar. As she knelt in prayer, she felt as if her surroundings were embracing her; they were so similar to the interior of the church of her childhood in Cooperstown, and she felt at home.

It was a quick stop. She said a few prayers, and again, as she had done for the past sixteen hours, she begged for God's forgiveness for her sinfulness. When she emerged a few minutes later, she stood on the front porch before descending the stairs. After her eyes had adjusted to the sun's intensity, she walked to the car and drove back to camp. *Refocus, Chris,* she told herself. *Refocus!*

CHAPTER 10

Glad to be back after the vigorous hike, Chris climbed into the shower within minutes of her arrival. With her hair wrapped in a towel, she made her way to the bedroom. She hadn't remade the bed since she had climbed out of it in the middle of the night.

Maybe I'll take a quick nap, she thought.

As she stood naked in front of the mirror that sat atop the maple vanity, she noticed a few red blotches around her breasts and neck. Upon closer inspection she thought angrily, *Did Fred do this? I wonder how long I'll have visible reminders of last night.*

Chris stared at her naked frame, feeling very womanly, no longer like a girl. She ran her hands over the same breasts that Fred Taylor had caressed less than twenty-four hours ago.

How disgusting my behavior was, she thought, as she again remembered how she had felt as Fred pressed his body against hers.

It was so exciting, though…

As she took pleasure in the reflections of her tanned body, she was flooded with the teenage memory of a chilly Saturday afternoon in mid-November after a girlfriend's birthday party, when the smell of cigarette smoke hit her as soon as she opened the back door of their Cooperstown home. At their kitchen table, she saw her Aunt Charlotte sitting with her mom, enjoying coffee and apple pie on the Bavarian china plates, which Chris knew her mom only used for special occasions. Chris yelled, "Aunt Char!" and moved to her side, as her statuesque aunt rose from the wooden kitchen chair and gave her a hug. Chris reached into her pocket to grab a handkerchief and wipe her dripping nose. She unbuttoned her coat and hung it on the back of a chair next to her aunt, whom she learned had made the 140-mile trip from her home in Scranton, Pennsylvania. Spying the five butts in the ashtray, Chris figured she'd been there for a couple of hours.

It was rare to see her mother's sister, who only made the four-hour trip once or twice a year. Chris admired her aunt, who looked like she had stepped out of the pages of *McCall's Magazine* and always appeared ready for a photo shoot.

She was now giving Chris the once-over and admiring her pretty pink party dress. "My, Chris," she said, "you are really growing up."

A little self-conscious, Chris, who was still bubbling over with excitement from the party, told her mom and aunt about the other classmates who were there, the tasty snacks they'd eaten, and the delicious birthday cake. She paused for a moment then added, "Mom, did you know Linda's older sister went to Albany to finish out her junior year? She wasn't there today at the party, and when I asked about her, Mrs. Thorpe said she'd gone to live at a Catholic boarding school for the rest of the year."

With that said, Chris noticed the two sisters staring at each other, but she charged ahead. "When I asked why, they sort of changed the subject. I can't understand why she'd go away. She's so popular and a good student too. I asked Linda about it later when I got ready to leave, but she just said her parents had decided it was the best place for her."

Chris watched as Aunt Charlotte, rather dramatically, held her cigarette in her fingers, which sported bright-red polish. Always one to confront the reality of situations, her aunt confidently reported, "She's probably in a motherly way."

Chris, a little unsure of exactly what that meant, was quick to respond, "What do you mean by 'a motherly way'?"

Without hesitation, Aunt Charlotte turned to her sister and, looking aghast, said, "Mary, do you mean to tell me you haven't told Christine the facts of life?"

At hearing the phrase "the facts of life," Chris was all ears. She was always seeking out any information she could about sex. The subject, Chris had discovered, was taboo around her house and those of many of her friends as well. Frequently her girlfriends had huddled in the back of the classroom when one of them had acquired a spicy new tidbit of information.

But now, as Chris observed her mother taking a long drag on her cigarette, she listened to her words as they rode out on a puff of smoke. "Charlotte, Christine knows she is a chaste young woman and is aware she's not to be alone with boys who might take advantage of her. She knows she needs to remain a virgin until she's married."

Chris angrily thought, *She's never said that to me before. If she wanted me to know that, why hasn't she told me?*

Still, she hoped the conversation would continue. With Aunt Char present, she was learning more about being a woman than she could have hoped. It therefore came as a great disappointment when the conversation dissolved into her mother urging her to change out of her party dress and get ready to help with dinner.

The effects of that day, however, were sewn into Chris's moral fabric. When Linda's sister, Kathy, returned to school for her senior year, it was whispered that she had borne a child out of wedlock and given it to the good sisters for adoption, which allowed her to return to her hometown and family. What Chris remembered most, however, was the life that followed for Kathy, and she vowed never to get herself into that situation. Kathy was now shunned, talked about behind her back, and viewed by many as a Hester; Chris wouldn't walk around with a scarlet letter on her chest like that.

How easy it was in those days for me to look at another young woman and label her, Chris now thought. *What about me? Aren't I the same kind of sinner? Having sex outside of marriage? On the other hand, wasn't my "episode" with Fred sex between two consenting adults?*

Turning around to climb into bed, she stared at the Indian maiden in the painting that hung on the wall. The young woman wore an animal hide, with a single feather rising heavenward from her headband, as she glanced up at the magnificent pine trees that lined what appeared to be an Adirondack creek on whose bank she stood. *The Spirit of the Forest* had hung over this bed for as long as Chris could recall, yet it never had seemed to provide the comfort it did today, as if someone—a single woman like her—were watching out for Chris, alone in these mountains.

Why couldn't she have been there last night to keep this from happening? Chris asked herself. *But do I really wish it never happened?*

Her body hit the cool sheets as she lay down, and her immediate thought was the sensation she'd felt when Fred had put her down on his bed the night before. She simply could not escape the memory, the emotion, and the feelings. How different, pleasant, and refreshing this bed was for her.

After an hour she awoke refreshed, dressed quickly, and put her hair into a bun at the nape of her neck. She grabbed the pile of dirty clothes in her room, carried them to the kitchen sink, put in the stopper, and filled the sink with water that was as hot as she could stand. She decided to let the clothes soak.

She was ravenous and thankfully remembered a package of spaghetti and meatballs she had frozen and brought along with her to camp.

An hour later, dinner completed and clothes washed and hung out to dry, she decided to take a short canoe trip. The temperature was still comfortable, perhaps in the midseventies, and she thought she could do without a sweater or sweatshirt. She found her life preserver in a chair on the front porch, where apparently she had tossed it upon her return last night.

She approached the canoe, thinking, *At least I wasn't too drunk last night to forget to tie it up.*

As she walked to the first of two aluminum docking cleats where she had secured the canoe, her eyes caught sight of a small rock on the dock.

How did that get there? she asked herself in bewilderment.

She walked over and noticed a slip of paper poking out from beneath it. She lifted the rock, tossed it to the shore, and removed the piece of paper. As she stood back up, she opened the folded white notebook paper and read.

Chris,

    I recognized your canoe, so I decided to stop and see how you were. No one was here, so thought I'd leave this note. Missed you stopping by for coffee this morning. So glad you came for dinner last night. It was wonderful. Sorry you left so soon. Didn't know what your plans were and if we might get together again. Stop by for coffee tomorrow morning.

Fred

You've got to be kidding me, Chris thought. *I don't believe it. He's got a hell of a lot of nerve.* She was furious as she stared at the note. *When did he come here? Was it while I was in Inlet this morning or when I was out hiking?* She was grateful she had locked up the camp, something she rarely did.

Why wasn't I here when he came? I would have gotten to see him one more time.

Examining the paper she concluded that he must have brought along a tablet and pen, as he had no way of knowing whether she'd be there. The top of the page was ragged, torn from a spiral ring notebook.

He certainly took some time to plan this, she figured, thinking about his strategy.

Since her return from Fred's camp last night, this was the first time she had felt his physical presence, almost as if she were being spied upon, being stalked, which made her feel uncomfortable.

Well, he obviously remembered where the camp was and found it without much difficulty, she thought. *Will he stop by again?*

She stuffed the note into her shorts pocket, put on the life jacket, untied the ropes, and stepped into the craft. Within minutes she was heading across the lake.

Earlier she had heard the loons, and the noises sounded, from the direction of their calls, as if they were coming from the pair that nested on Sixth Lake. She was heading their way.

She paddled into the large bay off to her right. There were only a few camps there, and she pulled carefully into a secluded area that was filled with downed trees and stumps. The depth of the water in the inlet was only eight or ten inches. She pulled the paddle from the water and laid it across the gunnels.

Mom and Dad, where are you when I need you? she asked pleadingly. *If I'd invited you to come along with me here, none of this would be happening.* But once again she contradicted herself. *Am I glad that I'm at camp alone,* she wondered, *so I can do what I want and no one will know but me?*

"Put the questions to rest for a little bit, Chris. Relax and enjoy," she said out loud. For the next fifteen minutes, she tried to calm the ongoing battle within. She basked in the sounds of the loons, the slight breeze rustling the leaves of the dense green hardwoods, and the language of the mountains.

I don't know why I should be scared or frightened if Fred comes back, she thought. *He obviously has a different understanding of what happened last night. He thinks I'm nice. His note indicated he wants to see me again. Perhaps I'm overreacting.*

Chris paddled gently back to camp as a cooling breeze replaced the heat of day. The bright golden sun had set, and her canoe trip took just fifteen minutes.

As she walked up to the camp, she disturbed the seven or eight ducks that had settled on the grass. They quickly reassembled after she passed, settling in for the night. As Chris looked back, she thought that she should follow their example. *I should react the same way. I may be disturbed temporarily, but no one is going to upset my life.*

She seemed to have gained some insight from all the questions she had asked herself. The events of last night had been far too dramatic—and frankly traumatic—for her to think she could resolve them in a single day. She remembered her dad often repeating the words, "Time is a wonderful healer," and she resolved to focus on that.

Her sleep, a few hours later, was restless, and tossing and turning, she thought perhaps she had overdone the hiking, climbing, cleaning, and canoeing over the past three days. Her body was rebelling. Thoughts of Fred Taylor filled her head, and she couldn't rid herself of them. *How long will I have to suffer from these thoughts?* she wondered. *I can't believe I participated and enjoyed it.*

She played out the questions again and mentally worked hard at not purchasing a ticket for the guilt trip she seemed to want to take.

Fred was the perpetrator, the aggressor, she told herself. *Did I have a choice?* And then she again wondered, *Why didn't I scream? That would have brought the attention of neighbors.*

She thought of all the actions she might have taken to prevent her assault and somewhere in the midst of it knew it was hindsight. She hadn't made any moves to stop him.

Move on, Chris, she thought. *I hope that Dad was right and that time will take care of this.* Her body relaxed, easing the tension, and she succumbed to sleep.

She arose bright and early and walked to the front window of the camp to check the temperature on the porch thermometer. It registered a chilly fifty degrees. That, plus the soreness of her muscles, persuaded Chris to forego her daily canoe trip and the possibility of running into Fred.

She donned a pair of jeans and a sweatshirt and looked for slippers to keep her feet warm. She grabbed a banana from the bowl atop the fridge, along with a cup of freshly brewed coffee, and headed to the dining room table. Yesterday's paper still lay there; she turned to the funny pages and started the crossword puzzle. This too was part of the camp experience, the opportunity to laze around. She could eat breakfast at her leisure, do puzzles, enjoy a cup of coffee, and not feel guilty about any of it. She could relax and simply enjoy the peace and quiet.

She wondered whether there were any major news stories since she had read yesterday's paper; she momentarily thought about turning on the old portable radio that sat on the kitchen shelf. The signal was so poor, however, that the only time she really listened to it was in the evening when she could pick up WQXR out of New York City. She reminded herself that this is why one came to camp, for the peace and quiet. When she was a child, her dad always had said, "A little solitude never hurt anyone."

Having finished the crossword, breakfast, and four cups of coffee, she was revved and ready to go. This was the preplanned day that she had agreed to spend with her and David's good friends who, like her, also were vacationing in the Adirondacks.

An hour later, having traveled eight miles along South Shore Road, the route that runs along the back side of the first four of the Fulton Chain of Lakes, she spotted the sign her friends had told her to look for. She made the right hand turn at LAIRD'S LANDING and followed the narrow dirt driveway through pines and hardwoods for about a quarter-mile. Chris was grateful for the carefully printed directions as several spokes that led to other camps cropped up along the way. She found her destination without difficulty and parked her car.

Patty, wearing her familiar tie-dyed full-length dress, bounded out of the camp. Chris handed her a bottle of wine she'd purchased on her way. They linked arms as they walked into the kitchen, where Ken said, "How ya doin', sister?" It was his usual greeting.

Five years into Chris's newspaper career, Ken had come on board as a sportswriter at the paper. He recently had begged the newspaper's editors to send him to Montreal to cover the Summer Olympics there and had just returned.

Patty was a librarian and, as Chris would say, a free spirit. Chris was drawn to them because of their eccentricities and often commented that they were "flower children" before the term was popular. Chris often called Patty a thin Mama Cass.

"How's your week going, Chris?" Ken inquired.

Without hesitation she responded, "Fine."

"What have you been up to?"

She spent the next five minutes discussing her hike up Blue Mountain, her daily canoe outings, and her hike at Raquette Lake the day before.

"Have you talked to David?" he asked.

Oh, my God, thought Chris. *I should have called him when I stopped in Inlet.*

Quickly she responded, "I called him yesterday, and all seems well. He knows there's no phone at camp. I'll probably call him from a payphone when I go back through Inlet."

"Why don't you call him from here?" Ken said. "There's a phone in the living room. Besides, I'd like to know just how much everybody misses me at the paper."

"OK, let's do it," Chris said, as Ken and Patty led her into the living room, a small area with a huge picture window that overlooked the lake.

As Chris dialed the number, she wasn't quite sure what to say. She still was wrestling with herself over her encounter with Fred and hoped David would do most of the talking. He picked up on the fourth ring, and Chris said a simple, "Hello."

David's immediate response was, "Chris, how are you doing? I was hoping to hear from you today."

"I'm here with Ken and Patty. Ken wants to know if he's missed at the paper," Chris said.

"You both are," David reported. "Especially you, Chris. I can't begin to tell you how much I've missed you. And the kids want to know when you're coming home so we can have you over to the house. I think we need to talk seriously about tying the knot. Think about it, please," he pleaded.

"I will David. This week has given me time and space to do a lot of soul searching. Yes, we'll talk when I get back."

Chris handed the phone to Ken, hoping she had placated David for the moment. With all the issues she'd been dealing with over the past thirty-six hours, she hadn't spent serious time thinking about a forthcoming engagement.

Can I move forward with a marriage to David and forget all about what happened this week? she thought.

The guys chatted for a few minutes, and Ken handed the receiver back to Chris.

"David, I think I'll be home on Friday and not wait for my parents' arrival on Saturday. I'll give you a call when I get home. Please don't worry. I'm at camp, and everything's fine," Chris offered, trying again to appease him.

"I love you, Christine Wright. Hurry home," David said, with longing and a bit of sadness in his voice.

Patty encouraged Chris and Ken to join her on the front porch, where she had set out a tray of coffee, sliced fresh fruit, and blueberry muffins. They sat in white wicker chairs with lovely floral seat pads, and they pulled their chairs around the small matching table to enjoy the provisions Patty had spread before them. The day was warming rapidly, and the breeze proved most welcoming.

They spent the next three hours in conversation, debate, and laughter. Ken talked about his many Olympic adventures; Patty discussed her library work and some of the new adult and children's programs she was putting into place for the fall. Chris added her approval to Patty's plans.

She was present in body, but her thoughts lingered on Fred, as she wondered, *When he didn't see me this morning canoeing by his dock, did he come looking for me? Is he rowing his boat to our camp right now?*

"Chris, are you all right?" Patty commented. "You seem a million miles away."

Unsure how to respond, she said, "David has really been pushing the idea of getting married. He asked me again when we were on the phone. I'm probably just a bit preoccupied with his proposal."

"That's wonderful," Patty said. "You and David are such a great twosome, and we know how much you love his kids. You'd be such a great stepmom. Think about it, Chris. They don't come any better than David. But you already know that."

Her positive, encouraging words about their relationship elicited deep feelings of distress with Chris. *How would Patty, Ken, and dear David react if they knew about my one-night stand with a married man?*

Later on they walked down to the dock. Patty excused herself after a bit to whip up some stir-fry. She returned twenty minutes later with plates, utensils, and stir-fry tucked into a picnic basket. She served her creation, and Chris commented on the delightful taste and selection of sliced vegetables. That's what she loved about these two; they were a bit unpredictable. No hot dogs for them on a summer afternoon.

It was getting close to three thirty. Chris felt exhausted, as if she'd been swimming against the current all day, making no headway in the raging waters of her mind. She made the excuse that she wanted to get back to camp so she could take her daily canoe trip she'd put off this morning. She wasn't sure whether or not she was being truthful. Today was the first time since the sexual incident that she'd had a conversation with people she knew, and she felt conspicuous, as if the world were pointing its finger at her and saying, "Adulteress, fornicator, whore." She felt uncomfortable and would have used almost any excuse to return to Lake Wrights.

Her dear friends sensed her need to be in her own space for a while. Good-byes were shared with the hope that the following week they'd get together when everyone returned home.

Once Chris's car was back on South Shore Road, she wondered, *Am I always going to feel like this? Even after I go to confession, will I still see myself as a sinner?*

She felt guilt-laden at her own choices, her own behavior, and the image of herself. Anger rose in her once again as she directed all blame toward Fred.

Why did you do this to me? Why did you have to ruin what was going to be a relaxing week at camp, one where I could feel refreshed and renewed? It's like you threw a pail of muddy water all over me. I hate you, Fred Taylor.

In anger she beat the steering wheel with her fist. Shortly her focus reverted to the task at hand—returning safely to camp. She felt overwhelmed by the emotions of the past three days: bitterness, confusion, shame.

Stop putting yourself through this trauma, Chris, she demanded of herself.

As she neared Inlet, she took note of two does as they grazed along the side of the road. She slowed almost to a stop and passed carefully. As many times as she saw these animals in their native habitat, it still took her breath away. She remembered her dad sharing another of his many Adirondack stories.

"Thank God for those men sixty or seventy years ago who saw the North Woods as the gem it is and urged the legislature to create an Adirondack Forest Preserve," Hal Wright had fondly expressed.

Chris reflected momentarily on the many stories her dad had told the family over the years—stories she couldn't forget. Right now she was thankful for all of them; they diverted her attention from her mental turmoil.

By the time she withdrew the keys from the ignition, her decision was made. She might hate Fred Taylor and feel terrible about the events earlier in the week, but it wouldn't change the way she felt about these mountains or this camp or the lake. This place had been her home away from home since she was eight, and nothing—absolutely nothing—would change that.

I'll stay until tomorrow and enjoy every minute of it! she vowed.

She unlocked the back door, which seemed so strange and out of character. *When was the last time any of us locked up camp while we were staying here, whether we went hiking for the day or out to dinner?*

But she knew she felt much more comfortable doing so. She tossed the car keys onto the kitchen counter, grabbed a can of soda from the refrigerator, and headed to the front door. After unlocking it, she pulled it open and pushed an old flatiron that was used as the doorstop in front of it.

"I don't believe it," she uttered, as she glanced up and spied Fred Taylor sitting in one of the Adirondack chairs at the end of her dock. He was turned sidewise, so she only saw his profile, but she had no doubt it was him. Plus she spotted his rowboat; it was pulled up on shore just past her canoe.

Does he know I'm home? Did he hear me pull in? I'd better confront him before he walks up here, she decided. *It's the middle of the day. People are all over their docks and in the water. If he does anything, I'll scream.*

Another voice inside her said, *It'll be good to see him again. I wonder what he'll have to say.*

Chris walked out the front door, allowing it to slam shut, giving Fred fair warning that she was heading his way. She clearly had gotten his attention, as she saw him turn and rise from the chair. He was heading toward her. She quickened her pace and met him as he neared the end of the dock. He was barefoot, dressed in red swimming trunks and a white T-shirt.

"Chris, how good to see you. I began to think you might already have left to go home. I've missed having coffee with you in the morning," Fred said.

Chris, looking directly at him and keeping her distance at about six feet, demanded, "Mr. Taylor, I don't ever want to see you again. I think you'd best leave our dock and row back to your camp."

She surprised herself, wondering how she had summoned the courage to speak to Fred in this manner.

Fred started to approach her, but Chris quickly responded by moving sideways, away from him.

"What's the matter, Chris? And what's with the 'Mr. Taylor' bit?"

Chris spoke from an unemotional, neutral platform, which she had quickly conceived in her mind. "Your actions were uncalled for. You plied me with alcohol and then took advantage of me against my will. You're old enough to be my father, for God's sake, and you should know better."

"Whoa. Wait a minute, Chris. Don't get so excited. We had a little sex. You seemed to be a willing partner. What's the big deal? We're both adults, and the sex was great. Wouldn't you agree?"

Chris couldn't believe it. It was as if they were communicating from two different planets, with two entirely different understandings of what had occurred.

Or does Fred remember the events as they really happened? she wondered. *What am I trying to deny?*

"Mr. Taylor, I'm only going to say this once more. Please leave, and don't come back. You've got one hell of a nerve to plop yourself down on our dock. No one invited you, and no one ever will. You leave now, or I'm going to scream. Try to explain that when everyone responds to my shouts."

Chris was trying her best to stay in control, but she felt the anger rise within her and knew her face was red; she could sense the warmth.

She was well aware of her attempts to absolve herself of any blame. She somehow, in some way, needed to convince Fred that she hadn't been a willing partner in his sexual tryst; it had all been his idea, his plan. She wouldn't believe her behavior at his camp had caused her to sin and wasn't about to accept that what had transpired was her choice.

Fred turned, stopped, and softly said, "I don't know where your head is, Chris. All I know is that you accepted my invitation. I didn't force you to drink, and I certainly didn't force you to make love. You were pretty receptive and seemed to enjoy it. I'll leave it there. Obviously you think differently. But I don't think I'm wrong in what I remember of the night. Good luck to you, Chris."

He moved toward the green rowboat, pushed it into the water, and waded to a point where he stepped up and into it and then sat down. As he dropped the oars into the water and began to row, he kept a bead on Chris, but she tried to ignore him.

Realizing her body was trembling, she walked onto the dock. She questioned whether her strong statements to Fred were in fact what she wanted to say. *It was what I had to do,* she concluded as she repositioned the chairs.

Once he was out of sight, Chris returned to the camp, made herself a Manhattan, grabbed her novel, and returned to the porch, where she thought she could finish up the last few chapters of *Centennial.* She gave reading her best shot but discovered she couldn't concentrate and found, after taking ten minutes to turn a page, that this distraction wasn't going to work.

She desperately wanted her parents here to comfort and protect her. She felt she needed to share with her dad the way Fred Taylor had treated her. *After all,* she mused, *I am Daddy's little girl.* Even so, she knew that never would happen. *What would he say? How would he react?* Chris wondered.

"You had sex with a married man?" would be his response.

Chris laid the book on the porch and slowly sipped her drink as she made plans about the rest of her life, or at least the next day or two. She finished the drink and tidied up the camp. Her plan at the moment was to enjoy one last canoe ride in the morning, pack up her clothes and the little bit of food she wanted to take home, and be on the road to Clinton by late morning.

The next morning, as planned, with the car packed, the canoe pulled up on shore, and everything at camp in its proper place, Chris did a last-minute walkthrough, knowing she didn't want to disappoint her mom by not leaving camp exactly as she had found it. Her mother had set a high standard. The only thing left to do was close the door on the sordid events of the past week.

The sun, directly overhead, shone down on the driveway as Chris put her Chevy hatchback into drive. She hoped she would make it to the road and be well out of sight before Fred—who might be lurking out there, waiting for such an opportunity—might confront her again. She wanted to leave him and every memory of him in the dust she was kicking up.

As the car hit Route 28, she was happy that at the last minute she had remembered to re-hang the camp sign. She knew her dad would question its whereabouts if she hadn't put it back in place. As she headed west, she was pleased that she didn't see Fred anywhere in her rearview mirror.

Really, Chris? You heard what he said yesterday. He's not stalking you. He only saw you as a willing partner.

"Did I really think he'd be lying in wait for me when I pulled out?" she said out loud, wondering whether she'd read too many mystery novels. She breathed a sigh of relief and decided to put all her questions to rest. Any and all encounters with Fred Taylor were over. She was on her way home.

A mile down the road, she pushed the buttons on the dash, trying to find something worth listening to on the radio. No matter the station, it appeared that "Afternoon Delight" was the song of the moment.

Just what I need, she thought.

"Skyrockets in flight, afternoon delight..." The Starland Vocal Band's summer hit wasn't helping.

Keep moving the dial. There's got to be something else, she thought. Softer, gentle strains finally emerged from the speakers—a classical station playing a personal favorite of hers, Dvořák's symphony *From the New World*, and she thanked God for music that soothed her anxious spirit.

A half-hour later, with the noonday sun pouring its light and heat down, she descended the hill toward Moose River. As she drove over the McKeever Bridge, she took a deep breath as she sang, "Like a bridge over troubled water..." and thought, *I'll be home in a little over an hour. Forget the memories of the week, Chris. Stay positive.*

She relaxed and concentrated on her driving, only now relaxing the grasp she had on the steering wheel, and thought, *Not to worry, Chris. Everything will be fine.*

CHAPTER 11

Chris couldn't remember driving most of the familiar route as she neared her home for the past ten years in Clinton, New York. Her mind had been focused on reliving and replaying the events of the past week. She was well aware that she hadn't been concentrating on her driving and felt grateful that she had returned home safely. Within the sphere resting on Chris's shoulders were so many varying scenes that it was impossible for her to simultaneously direct all of them as they popped up on her brain's sound stage.

She drove her white Chevy along the maple-lined main street, typical of the villages in the area, and turned slowly into the gravel driveway of the large blue Victorian house where she occupied the entire second floor. It was early Friday afternoon, and she realized she had left for the Adirondacks just last Sunday. However, for Chris, as she now returned to a comfortable and everyday world, her time away seemed so much longer. She felt as though a lifetime of events had unfolded in the past six days.

Chris recalled how she and Mike had practically drooled when they'd read the ad for this apartment rental a decade ago and jumped at the chance to lease it. They found it absolutely divine—freshly painted, ample room to spread out, an office for Mike, and a spare bedroom that Chris was certain could accommodate a table, electric typewriter, and bookshelves.

It was just a little after one in the afternoon. She unpacked her suitcase as well as a cardboard box of laundry and a bag of foodstuffs. When she had unlocked the back door to the flat, her nostrils filled with the mustiness of the place, as it had been shut off from fresh air for nearly a week. She opened the full-length white drapes in the living room and raised the windows to allow cooler breezes to rush in. Chris and Mike were always grateful that the mighty maple trees that surrounded the property provided the comforting breath of fresh air in the heat of summer, especially since the apartment had no air conditioning.

She undressed and took a cool bath, then slipped into a light, sleeveless print dress and a pair of white sandals. Sitting at the kitchen table, she sorted through a week's worth of mail she had picked up at the post office on her way home.

This'll help me buy some new fall clothes, she speculated, as she looked at the two checks that had been folded inside acceptance letters for articles she had submitted for magazine publication.

Over the years Chris always questioned the method or madness behind the selection of her submissions. Some she thought were well written, timely, and matched the requested word count yet were never accepted; on the other hand, she had dashed off some in record time just to meet a deadline, and those had been accepted. The one thing she never questioned was when a publisher sent her compensation for her work. In so many ways, it was visible proof of her skills and talent. She embraced the written word, and if she could be paid for doing what she loved, what else mattered?

She stood up and straightened the mess on the table, tossing empty envelopes and undesired mail into the wastebasket, and thought, *Now what?*

She knew she needed to let her folks know she was home and wouldn't be at camp when they planned to arrive there the next day. So she headed into the living room and dialed her parents' number. As the phone rang, she stood surrounded by the golden rays of the late-afternoon sunlight that now filled the room.

I so wish this sunny glow could be my interior light, she thought.

Mary Wright answered after a few rings, and Chris explained that she had come home a bit early. She detected disappointment in her mom's voice.

"I got my fill of canoeing and hiking and really wanted to get back to see David and the kids," Chris explained. "Maybe we can all be there for Labor Day weekend," she offered, as an appeasement for disappointing them.

"How was your week? Did everything go all right? It sounds like you did everything you set your sights on doing," Mary asked.

"I did, Mom, and I cleaned the camp, just as I'd hoped to do. It looks good. I think you'll like the results. I even washed the curtains. Have a great week at camp. I'll talk to you when you get back."

After her mother said good-bye, Chris hung up and quickly dialed David's number at work, knowing he'd be anticipating a call once she arrived home. He couldn't have sounded happier when he recognized her voice. "Chris, are you still at camp?"

"No, I got home a little while ago," Chris said, as she nervously played with the phone cord. "I really missed you and thought we could have dinner at your house tomorrow night. I could be there by five."

"Oh, Chris. That's great. But what about tonight?"

Whether it was an authentic explanation or a lame excuse, she said, "You know, I'm still trying to get caught up on mail. I still have to do laundry, and I need to do some grocery shopping."

"All right then. We'll make it tomorrow. I'll barbecue some chicken, if that sounds good to you."

"That'll be fine. See you at five."

As Chris ambled back to the kitchen, she gave thought to her motivations; did she just want to get away from Fred Taylor?

Had he not been there, would she have stayed longer and enjoyed some special time with her parents, or did she really miss David and his children? It seemed to all be a jumble inside her head.

She decided to wash a load of dirty clothes she had brought from camp. As she threw her clothing into the washer, she vented her anger, heaving and tossing each piece at an imagined Fred Taylor.

When she exited the small back room where the machines sat, she decided to type up the bicentennial article she had completed at camp; hopefully she'd be able to mail it out today. She sat typing at her desk, which she had relocated—along with her bookcase, worktable, and electric typewriter—to the office Mike had used for the last eight years. An hour later, when the clock read four thirty, she realized she had just a half-hour to make it to the post office before closing time. She addressed the manila envelope that contained the article, took a quick inventory of her grocery needs, moved the wash into the dryer, and decided she'd walk to the post office and the grocery store.

The afternoon air, though quite warm, felt dry and fresh; she breathed it in deeply. *Maybe the walk will do me some good, clear my brain, and allow me to think new thoughts. Maybe it'll smooth out the ruffled surfaces of my soul and mind.*

Although her hope was to rid her mind of her recent days at camp, she replayed her conversation from the day before when she basically had kicked Fred off the property.

I can't believe I actually confronted him like that, she told herself proudly, thinking back on her strong words. She was still haunted, however, by his words, when he had tried to explain an event that she had viewed through a very different set of lenses.

Quickly and steadily she walked down the familiar main street and mailed her envelope. Mr. Griffin, the postmaster, sorting a stack of mail on the counter, looked up at Chris. "Nice to see you twice in one day, young lady."

Chris smiled, acknowledging his comment. She was home.

After picking up some groceries, she approached St. Mark's, the Roman Catholic Church she and Mike regularly had attended. As she walked up the front steps, she hoped that perhaps the door might be unlocked. A smile crossed her face as she reached for the pull on the massive front wooden door and found that it opened easily. She walked inside to the seventh pew from the front, on the right-hand side, where Mike and she always had sat.

After placing her grocery bags on the pew, she knelt. Looking toward the altar, she wondered just how she should begin her prayer after what she considered to be her evening of sin and shame. *What was I thinking to have let this happen? Oh, God, I am so sorry.*

Rather than allow herself to remain in prayer, she suddenly seemed to know exactly how to handle her discomfort. *I believe I can put this whole situation to rest,* she thought, as she gazed out at the sanctuary. *I'll leave a little early tomorrow on my way to see David and the kids and stop by St. John's Church and go to confession with Father Jim.*

Chris sat for another few minutes, doing more planning than praying. As she exited the cool, dimly lit space, she shielded her eyes as they adjusted to the sunlight.

When she returned home, she unpacked the groceries and folded the laundry and put it away. She then decided on a quick tuna salad for dinner. The rest of her evening, as she now relaxed in a green caftan, was spent taking care of bills that had arrived and reading circulars regarding upcoming events on the neighboring college campus as well as in the Central New York area. She read the latest issue of *Time* magazine and a copy of *Adirondack Life,* thinking that she was back to normal and feeling positive about the day to come.

The next day, around four in the afternoon, dressed in a sleeveless, floral dress, with white sandals and a matching purse, she was off to Utica, a quick nine-mile drive. On this summer Saturday, there didn't appear to be too many cars downtown, and she easily parked on the street near the front of the old brick church. As she entered St. John's, she saw the line of penitents. With Father Jim and his assistant pastor both hearing confessions, she knew the wait wouldn't be long.

David had introduced Chris to Father Jim O'Connor when, soon after she had started to write for the paper, he was present at a community gathering. He was David's new pastor and had made an impression on him because of his extreme involvement in the community. Chris admired his activism and felt he understood the documents of the Second Vatican Council better than anyone she had encountered and that he was doing his best to carry out its teachings.

As she covered the political scene in those days, Chris frequently crossed paths with him. It wasn't long before she asked him if she could meet with him regularly for spiritual guidance. He had consented, and for the past eight years, once a month, they had met one on one. She loved his style, although, after a particularly meaningful session, she frequently noted that she had done all of the talking. She discovered that the art of spiritual direction resided in being an active listener.

A short while later, she stepped into the confessional. As she knelt, waiting for Father Jim to hear her confession, she thought that although she had a grievous sin to confess, she could think of no one with whom she had a better rapport than her spiritual director.

Her heart pounded as the wooden door slid open. Chris made the sign of the cross and said, "Father, it's Chris Wright. I was here a month ago, and I have sinned. Father Jim, I spent the past week at our camp in the Adirondacks. I met an older man there, the father of a boy I loved nineteen years ago. I had sex with the man; I'm not sure it wasn't rape. I didn't want to do it. He forced himself on me. But I'd accepted his dinner invitation at his camp, which I probably shouldn't have. I certainly didn't think he'd do anything like this, Father. I didn't think he'd take advantage of me. He's married and old enough to be my father. I hate him, Father, for what he did to me."

Chris took a deep breath, and Father Jim remained quiet and in listening mode on the other side of the screen. Chris continued, "I know I'll never have occasion to see this man again. I am deeply sorry for having committed these sins." For Christine Wright, at that moment, the weight had been lifted; she felt relieved.

There was silence. Chris was sure he had heard her. She could see him faintly through the screen. Finally Father Jim spoke. "How are you feeling, Chris?"

She thought, *What does he mean? How am I feeling? Guilty! What else?* She said nothing.

The priest leaned toward the opening. "Chris? How do you *feel?*"

"I know, I know. I heard you," she said softly in exasperation, although she wanted to scream. "I'm feeling *guilty*, Father. I know what's right and wrong, what's sinful and not. I had sex with a man, even if I was an unwilling partner."

"What drew you into the trap, Chris?"

"I'm not sure. He was handsome; he reminded me so much of Carl, his son, whom I loved when I was a teenager. He treated me nicely; we enjoyed each other's company; and we had coffee a couple of mornings on his dock when I was out canoeing. You know, Father, you've been there for me all through my separation and divorce from Mike. Maybe I was vulnerable. Maybe I played into his little game. I know the night it happened he gave me a couple of drinks, and then we had wine with dinner. I probably should have stopped after one drink. But even then, Father, I'm not so sure I could have stopped him. He seemed hell-bent on having sex. I told him not to. I told him to stop. He was powerful. I couldn't push him away."

"Chris, you had sex, whether you were a willing partner or not. You have great faith, and you know that our merciful God already has forgiven you. So you need to let go of it, as best you can. Move on, and know that God loves and forgives you. My question is, 'Can you forgive yourself?' "

She hesitated then slowly, recalling earlier conversations, said, "I do believe in an all-forgiving and merciful God, but I keep thinking about all our talks regarding the Sacrament of Matrimony before and during my marriage to Mike. How many times did I tell you I'd do anything to hold our marriage together? And now look what I've done to someone else's marriage. I don't know Fred's wife, but how would she feel about me if she found out I had sex with her husband? I can't think of a worse sin I've ever committed."

"I think a good penance for you, Chris, would be to put yourself in the care of the mother of Jesus. The Feast of the Assumption will be celebrated tomorrow. Perhaps you could dedicate your Mass to a personal renewal, a new step forward. Remember that your salvation was delivered through Mary. Perhaps you could say your Rosary in thanksgiving for her willingness to say 'Yes.' She proclaimed the greatness of the Lord. You should too. Now say an act of contrition, and I'll see you soon."

Chris did as directed, concluding with, "…to confess my sins, to do penance, and to amend my life. Amen." The door slid closed.

She pushed the deep-green velvet curtain aside as she walked out of the confessional. She retreated to a pew in front and, glancing at her watch, felt there was enough time for her to say the Rosary now. After finding her beads in an inside pocket of her purse, she knelt and began the familiar practice, praying for an interior peace.

The next few weeks were pleasant enough. Time with David and his children, get-togethers with Ken and Patty, productive time at work, and delight in some of her writing projects being accepted for publication were all quite satisfying.

There were special late-night dinners with David and an evening in late August that caught them both off-guard. They made love for the first time. As they lay in each other's arms, they wondered how it had come to happen. What had brought them to this intimate moment?

Giving Chris a tight embrace, David said, "Perhaps the time was right. Maybe the planets are perfectly aligned. What do you think?"

"All I know is that it was wonderful, David."

For a guilty moment, she thought about the last time she'd had sex with a man and how vastly different that occasion had been. She felt she had been right all along. Wasn't this how lovemaking was supposed to be—kind, gentle, loving? Their coming together in her bed had seemed so normal and natural and almost second nature, as if they'd both been in this place before. Lovemaking with David stood in such contrast to her sex with Fred, at least the encounter she had re-created in her own mind of their time together.

David had spoken to her throughout their lovemaking, repeatedly uttering soft expressions of "I love you" and "How wonderful you are" and "You are so beautiful"—words that brought a smile to her lips and joy to her heart.

It was open and honest, and although she knew that once again she was having sex outside of marriage, this was indeed very special. Everything she had hoped for in a husband she was discovering in this kind and gentle man who was so different from Fred Taylor. She still felt guilty, however. Over the past few weeks, she had done her best to put thoughts of Fred to rest, but periodically they floated to the forefront of her mind. Chris pondered whether to tell David about the encounter, but her shame and guilt and anxiety over his reaction kept her silent.

When her mom and dad had suggested she invite David and his children to join them at camp on Labor Day weekend, she happily extended the invitation. She knew this weekend would be profoundly different from her recent vacation. The memory of that week stayed with her, but with her relationship to David growing deeper and more intense, she was beginning to look forward to the trip. She felt a renewed hope in all the possibilities that this bond held for both of them.

If only it had gone that smoothly.

CHAPTER 12

Chris hadn't realized that for nearly an hour she'd been held captive by the decades-long secrets that haunted her—secrets she had buried that now were threatening the life she had meticulously created for herself and her family. She was aware that she had altered her position, at one point moving so that her back rested against a moss-covered white pine. This is where she now sat, her first thought being, *I've got to get back to camp before David and Ron get worried.*

When she reluctantly arose from what had become a dream space—a place she hadn't stepped into in a very long time—she held on to the memories as she carefully set the canoe free from its entrapment. Once clear of the rocks, she gingerly stepped into the canoe and departed the small bay. After lowering her hat over her eyes, she paddled directly into the afternoon sun.

Could this really have happened thirty-four years ago? she wondered. *I remember it as though it were yesterday.*

Chris, now paddling at an intense rate, caught herself working up a sweat. *Slow down,* she told herself. *Take pity on your sixty–eight year old body. Just get back to camp safe and sound.*

For the time being, she was at peace. She had relived, if only in her mind, her memories of Fred Taylor. She was willing to put them to rest, especially since he was dead. She could rest easy; the past was now in the past. The present was all that mattered.

She spotted David standing at the end of the dock, appearing to be on the lookout for her. Although she was a half-hour late, he'd be relieved that she was back safe and sound.

Stay in the moment, she thought, *and enjoy this last evening at camp.*

The following morning, Ron was up and out the door by eight. He gave his mother one last embrace; he was the master of the bear hug. "Sorry if I was too quiet at times. There's a lot going on in my head," he confessed to his mother.

"That's all right," Chris told him. "We all have a lot on our minds these days. Hopefully your time here helped you sort out some of your concerns."

"I can only hope. I don't ever remember doing this much stuff while we were at camp, Mom. I think all the diversions helped. But right now I need to get back to Utica to refocus and get back into the swing of things," he said, laughing. "It was a wonderful stay. I hope I didn't wear you and Dad out with all our traipsing around."

"It was fine, Ron. Your dad and I loved it. Have a safe trip home. I'll talk to you soon."

An hour later Chris and David, having finished cleaning up and packing, were also on the road home. Two-and-a-half hours later, when David drove into Cooperstown, he asked Chris if they should take the time to go to the post office and pick up the mail.

"We might as well pick it up now," she said. "You can run in."

Chris lowered her window as David parked and turned off the car. Minutes later he walked out and approached her open window and handed her the big bundle wrapped in a couple of huge red rubber bands.

"There's a certified letter for you on top," David said. "I had to sign for it."

Chris took a quick glance at the business envelope, noticing it was from a law firm she'd never heard of, and decided to wait until she arrived home to open it. She assumed it might have something to do with one of her recent magazine articles, perhaps a payment. Checks for published work were always welcome.

After they arrived home, David, who had been so meticulous in his packing of the vehicle, now did the unpacking; he dropped luggage, the ice chest, and a bag of dirty clothes just inside the back door. In the first few minutes after stepping into her kitchen, Chris did her best to put everything in its place, moving it out of the kitchen to be dealt with later.

She was about to prepare a pitcher of iced tea when she noticed the pile of mail. That would be her next chore. She placed the certified letter aside as she went through the circulars, magazines, and bills, dividing them all into "his" and "hers." The third pile she'd toss into the recycling bin. She found her letter opener in the small yellow box of pens and pencils on the marble countertop and sliced through the envelope. She saw that the return address was for a law firm in Cortland, New York. After grabbing the rest of her mail, she walked to the living room and sat in her favorite rose-colored velvet platform rocker. She placed the stack on an end table, withdrew the contents of the certified letter, and began to read.

Dear Chris,

You will be receiving this letter after my death, as I have instructed my attorney to do. Please do not be surprised that I know where you live and much of the details of your life.

In May 1977 I was in Utica to play an event with my combo. I picked up a copy of the local newspaper, hoping I'd catch your column, the one you talked so much about. What I found in the paper was a small article (one I've kept in my wallet all these years). It read, "Congratulations to Chris Wright and her husband David Herring on the birth of their son, Ronald. Chris's column, 'Around Town,' will return when she does."

I immediately remembered your telling me that David had a vasectomy, one of the reasons you were uncertain about marrying him. It didn't take too much math for me to realize it was just nine months since our time at Seventh Lake. Obviously you and David made some decisions and choices about your pregnancy, one being to let the world believe the child was his.

First let me thank you for bringing my son into the world. Thank you for never contacting me, not because I wouldn't have supported you and this child, but because I think it would have torn my marriage apart and devastated Carl.

Thank you for raising my son in such a way that he had a calling to the priesthood. (Although considering our first encounter, when I didn't want you to date Carl because you were Catholic, this is ironic. What do they say? Payback is a bitch!)

Yes, I know our son is a priest. I got my first computer in the midnineties and constantly did searches. And living in Cortland, a part of the Diocese of Syracuse, I saw the write-up and pictures in the paper when he was ordained.

How very proud you must be. I am too.
I got to meet him last year—not that he
knew it at the time. It was announced in the
paper that a visiting priest, Ronald Herring,
was giving a parish retreat at St. Bridget's
in Cortland. My wife Helen died in 2004, so
when I read about the event, I felt I could
go without someone questioning why I
would go to a Catholic church.

He really has a gift for public speaking.
My plan was just to go the first night, but
I wound up going all three evenings. I didn't
give him my name. I just shook his hand at
the end of each evening and told him how
much I enjoyed his talk. He obviously favors
you, but I was pleased at how much he
also resembles Carl.

Chris, Carl is the reason for this letter.
He's also receiving a letter that explains
everything. My reason for doing this is that
he has been diagnosed with leukemia and is
in need of a bone marrow transplant. I'm
hoping you will lean on our son Ron to be
tested to see if he is a match. I hope that
my two sons can meet and that Ron can
help his half-brother survive. I know this is
asking a lot, but perhaps, in some small way,
I can make things right for Carl. I took you
from him once. Now our son may give him
the chance to stay alive.

I am leaving this matter in Carl's hands.
I've included your address and phone number

in his letter. I believe he'll be in touch with you before long.

I'll rest easy, Chris, if you'll do what you can to help Carl recover from this horrible disease. Although you may not feel the same way, I'm glad that our lives converged when they did. I regret any pain and anguish I may have caused. I pray that God will guide you, Carl, and Ron in your upcoming discussions.

Fred Taylor

Still clinging to the white stationery in her right hand, Chris raised her left hand to her mouth, closed her eyes, and shook her head.

This cannot be happening, she thought. *Oh, God, what do I do now?*

She stared out through the sheer drapes that covered the front window and thought of the picture of Fred Taylor that had accompanied his obituary.

Why did he have to do this? Was it his one last dying wish? Why couldn't he have just left well enough alone?

Chris, speechless, wondered how she was going to share this letter with David, who had kept her secret all these years. She sat reflecting on Fred Taylor's last days and tried to imagine how he processed the options for his son's survival.

He must have thought of every possibility that might promote Carl's return to health. Contacting me couldn't have been his first choice.

She felt the anger rise in her chest—anger she hadn't experienced in a long time.

He must have run out of options. Oh, God, why?

Chris looked back at the letter, the words on the two pages, wondering when Fred had written it. There was no date.

He had to know his own death was imminent if he made the effort to write this letter and get it in the hands of his attorney, she thought. *He obviously was willing to do whatever it took to ensure Carl's survival.*

Chris leaned back in the rocker. *If Carl calls, what will he ask me? How much will he want to know about his father and me? Maybe in Fred's letter to Carl he explained everything. Carl may have more information than he needs or wants to know. Dear God!*

Chris was shaking. How would she deal with this information, this request? She reflected on her relationship with Carl; it had been pure and innocent, a coming-of-age moment in time, delightful and joy filled. And then her lovemaking with Fred filled her thoughts.

How is it possible that a relationship that began so guiltlessly with one member of a family wound up being so sinful with another?

Like so many times in her life, Chris's head burst with questions as she struggled to find answers. At this moment there were none. Her heart was pounding, and she became aware of the beating in her head. She looked back at the letter and slowly reread it, checking to see if she had missed anything.

Since there was no "I apologize" in the letter, apparently he never took responsibility for having sex with me against my will. What did he think happened that night?

It was in that very moment, with Chris's phrasing her words of anger and resentment, that, like a massive red velvet curtain rising on a stage, she viewed anew the sexual encounter she never had forgotten.

Over the years I've created my own reenactment of what occurred that evening, she thought. *I've never wanted to remember that I sinned. I know I've convinced myself that it was entirely Fred's fault, that I had no part in it. There wasn't any other way for me to think. Dad always said I was a good girl.*

Recalling their last conversation at the camp, Chris wondered whether Fred always had understood their sexual tryst differently. *Did I willingly accept his advances?*

Chris continued with her questions, and although she thought there were no answers, the responses all seemed so obvious to her at the moment. She realized that if she would simply allow herself to explore, once again, the scenario, that had led to the sexual encounter with Fred Taylor thirty-four years ago, she might find the answers deep within her heart and soul.

She reread the letter slowly. She felt that nothing was nuanced; it was perfectly straightforward. She raised her hands in prayer to her mouth. Her breathing became heavy, and she began to hyperventilate. Very slowly she uttered a mantra she regularly used in daily meditation, "My Lord. My God, My Savior, My All". She said it painstakingly, deliberately and slowed her breathing. Only when she felt in control did she rise from the rocker and walk back into the kitchen.

How can I keep this from David? she posited, knowing she and David hadn't kept secrets from each other during their years together.

David, his unpacking complete, had grabbed a dishtowel to wipe the perspiration from his face and neck. He uncapped a Saranac lager he'd set out on the table and slowly poured it into a pewter mug. He noticed his wife standing there, the letter dangling from her right hand.

He glanced up and, after taking a gulp of ice-cold beer, asked, "Is that the certified letter? What's it about?"

As reluctant as Chris was, she extended her hand, "David, you need to read this, and then we'll talk."

Moving toward the screen door where he'd have more light, he began to read. Chris knew this would take some time. Pacing wasn't her style, but she didn't feel like sitting down and waiting. She decided to make the iced tea she'd thought of earlier. Afterward she reluctantly sat down at the kitchen table.

"Well, I think we've got a problem here," David said, as he turned, heading back to the kitchen table. "We really need to talk this out." He laid the letter in front of Chris and, joining her at the table, pulled his beer mug in front of him.

Chris's immediate thought was, *He doesn't want to have to admit to Ron that he isn't his father. For thirty-four years, he's willingly and lovingly accepted Ron as his own.*

David began, "You know, Chris, yesterday when you were late getting back to camp, and I was so worried, you said you'd needed time to think about Fred Taylor's death. We both agreed that we'd gone over the situation countless times in the past thirty-some years. We agreed yesterday—and I don't feel any differently today—that no one needs to know that Ron isn't my son. I've put it to rest. How many more times do we need to rehash this?" He stood up, beads of perspiration forming on his brow. "Tell me, Chris. Do you really think I should tell Ron, after all these years, that he's not my son? I don't think so!" David seemed very firm in his resolve.

A long pause ensued; Chris sipped her iced tea, David his beer. Finally he turned to Chris as he paced the kitchen floor. "What are *you* thinking right now about this?"

Chris busied her hands, rubbing them together then making fists and tapping them against each other. "It sounds to me like there's a whole lot on our plates that we've got to chew on and try to digest over the next few days. I don't know when or if Carl may call, but we've got to be prepared for whatever he asks when he does. His survival is on the line. Wouldn't you agree? This has been *our* secret. You've never betrayed my decision. But never in my wildest dreams could I have imagined anything like this—that you and I would be forced to have to consider telling Ron that he has a half-brother who needs him."

David wiped his face and sat down opposite Chris, who became more intent on the questions she was asking. "Do you think we can deny Carl a possible bone marrow transplant if that's what Ron can provide? It could mean the difference between Carl's life or death."

David drank another beer, Chris another iced tea. The noontime air was hot and still.

"I think we need to focus on doing what's right," Chris continued, "even if it upsets you and me and Ron. There's a man out there who's dying. It certainly will be up to Ron to make his decision about that, but if we don't tell him the truth, it'll be one more secret kept, and I don't think we can keep doing that. Let's end this once and for all. We just need to think about the best way of doing it." Whether it was the heat or the conversation, David seemed hot and frustrated. "Let's go out on the porch," Chris offered. "Maybe we can catch a breeze."

They rose from the kitchen table and wandered through the foyer to the front porch.

"You know," David said, "I've often wondered after all these years if Ron hasn't figured perhaps something isn't right about my being his father. Our relationship has had its ups and downs, and he doesn't exactly look like me."

Chris quickly retorted with, "How could he know? He's never raised the issue. But maybe I'm just being naive."

Stepping out onto the front porch, Chris could see that it needed sweeping after being neglected for a week. It appeared that her brother Hal had seen to the watering of the hanging baskets, but their spent leaves and flowers littered the porch. Already knowing what Chris would ask, David quickly said, "I'll sweep up later."

It did set Chris's mind at ease, the house getting back to normal, cleaned up, everything in order. She sat down in the white slat rocking chair, and David took a seat in another. Folks were casually strolling along the sidewalk; Chris assumed they were tourists as they didn't look familiar, and she prided herself at recognizing most of the town residents. But at this moment, her thoughts were far from visitors to Cooperstown.

"In all honesty, David, I'm trying to figure out whether I'm relieved that the truth will finally come out, and this burden we've been carrying all these years will be lifted, or whether it would have been better if Carl had never needed Ron, and Fred had gone to his grave never having contacted me. It's like, right now, I have way too much information that I have to think about and process."

David quickly jumped in. "It isn't just you, Chris. This has always been *our* secret. And we both need to deal with it. I don't know what the right answer is. What I do know is that I don't want to lose the only son I have left, biological or otherwise."

Chris leaned back and rocked. How vividly she recalled the moment after they had become engaged when she had shared her maternity news with David; she also remembered his disbelief, disappointment, and angst. More precious were the memories when, after some lengthy soul searching, David had committed himself not only to marrying her but also accepting her unborn child.

"We've talked over the years, David. You know I've always felt that Ron should know his biological father. And yet neither of us could ever bring ourselves to tell him. He's only known you as his father, and you've been such a good one. Were we wrong to leave well enough alone?"

David stared off into space. He was in his own world.

Chris rose from her rocker and, placing her glass of tea on the small table between the two of them, turned to him. "For the last thirty-four years, this secret, this so-called sin I was hiding, always has been about protecting me from the shame of my getting pregnant out of wedlock with a married man. Even now it's distasteful for me to even say those words. But it happened, and you, rather than expose me to comments from friends and family, married me after my pregnancy was confirmed. I've probably made too many assumptions over the years, feeling you were fine with our decision. You've never complained, never thrown it in my face.

And for that I'm so grateful. You certainly weren't doing this for you; you already had Greg and DeEtte. You did it for me and Ron."

David, dishtowel still in hand, wiped his face. "I've stood by you all these years and have often said that this is *your* choice. But right now I'm not so sure. What will Ron think if we tell him? I love him and don't want to lose him. You're his mother—that's never going to change. But my relationship with him could change forever."

"We have time," Chris offered. "We can't be sure when Carl will call. Maybe he won't. We don't have to rush to make a decision."

It felt strange to Chris, the feeling of being in a position of acknowledging the truth. As difficult an issue as it was, she felt willing to come to grips with it; David apparently wasn't.

The afternoon air, although fragrant, was heavy and humid. Any refreshing breeze was absent. All Chris knew at the moment was that she still held the letter, the contents of which were going to change her life as she had intended it. She took a deep breath, perhaps to steady herself, knowing her world was being rocked.

The love of her life stood and wrapped his sweaty arms around her, as the first of what would be many tears shed over the ensuing weeks fell down their cheeks.

Looking into David's eyes Chris said, "I know this may sound strange, but I feel that everything will work out. Everything will be all right. As angry as I feel toward Fred for making this secret known to Carl, perhaps it's good for you and me to finally deal with it openly and honestly. I'll be so relieved if we can do that."

CHAPTER 13

Normalcy appeared to return to David and Chris's home, with both of them going about their routines. Each afternoon at four, as usual, Chris sought out her prayer space for the day, at this time of year choosing a comfortable chair on the back deck or front porch.

Ever since she had received Fred's letter and spoken with David about their dilemma, she could think of nothing else. She thought of Ron as a newborn baby asleep in her arms, and as a young man who had shared with his parents his call to the priesthood. When Ron was a young adult, there were so many occasions that had presented themselves, opportunities to tell him the truth about his birth father. Over the years, however, neither Chris nor David could bring themselves to reveal the truth. Now, as difficult as it was, they had to deal with that decision.

Ironically, David hadn't mentioned it since their initial conversation. It was clear to Chris that he didn't want to talk about it anymore.

She decided she needed a diversion and chose to concentrate on her late mother and father; daily prayer could help her focus on her memories of them. That way she wouldn't have to think about the letter and its contents.

Today, as she sat in prayer, she recalled how, as her mother had approached death in 1988, their relationship had grown deeper. Chris so wished that Mary Wright could magically appear right now in the chair next to her. Chris could play out this present scenario, asking, "Mom, what do *you* think? What would *you* do?"

A day hadn't passed without Chris praying for her mother, who had been diagnosed with lung cancer eleven months prior to her death. Although her early treatments had been hopeful, fifty years of smoking had taken their toll. During the last six weeks of her mother's life, Chris had driven daily from Utica to the home she and David now owned. Each trip had been a small trial. She had no regrets, however, and remained grateful for the precious time and intimate conversations she had with her mom in those waning days.

On many a drive alone, a voice inside her asked, *Do you want to share your secret with Mom before her death?* Chris thought long and hard about it, even discussing it at length with Father Jim. Once again she determined nothing could be gained by telling her mother about her experience with Fred Taylor.

Neither her mother nor father ever had questioned Ron being David's son. When he was born seven months after the wedding, they, like everyone else, just assumed she'd had premarital sex with David.

Chris often wrote articles and spoke publicly on the importance of honesty in writing, declaring that in journalism telling the truth is absolutely critical. Moments into her meditation, she noted how hypocritical she was being. *I can preach all I want about the truth,* she thought, *but when it comes to my sharing it—well, that's impossible.*

It wasn't that she hadn't wanted her folks to know what actually had happened. But she knew she couldn't live with the shame. She hadn't wanted to disappoint her parents, give them reason to see her as less than the proper young woman they had raised—no way!

When her mother had died, Ron was a happy, albeit precocious, sixth grader. Greg was a senior in college, and DeEtte was about to start her freshman year at Chris's alma mater. David and

Chris were very happy, and life was good. Why should Chris even contemplate making any changes to the status quo? So she didn't.

Her mother's funeral, a celebration of her life, took place at a crowded St. Mary's Church in Cooperstown. A day later the immediate family made its way to Seventh Lake. Hal Wright, Sr., had a plan.

Chris's sister Diane, having arrived from Long Island, and their brother Hal Jr., who still lived in Cooperstown, had packed up their families. They were all looking forward to the gathering; it was the first time they'd all be together in more than ten years at Lake Wrights. Hal, Sr., wasn't quite sure just where he would put all his progeny, but he knew that, with the use of cots and sleeping bags, they'd all be able to sleep comfortably. After all this was camp!

Everyone was looking forward to the reunion, especially after the pall that had been cast over them for the past several weeks. It was still hard for them to imagine Mary Wright gone at the age of seventy.

The gathering at Lake Wrights was far more than a family reunion. Her dad had arrived in advance, and by the time the caravan got there, the windows were open, coffee was brewing, and the canoe and rowboat were in the water and tied to the dock. He wanted to make everyone welcome.

Chris knew her father took great comfort in having all his children and grandchildren gathered about him. After such a loss and a year of his patient and loving care of his wife, this might very well have been the first time in almost a year that he was reasonably stress free.

When the doctors had determined that Mary's remaining time was short, Hal, Sr., had insisted that she come home from the hospital rather than go to a nursing home. Chris was still haunted by her father's sad face as he faithfully kept a bedside vigil, assisted by some caring nurses. She knew his own health was a growing concern; he had arthritic hands and knees, perhaps the result of almost sixty years of doing the grunt work of a laborer. He never complained, though. Chris knew he had loved the work of the lumber mill that had provided such a good living for their family.

She was glad for all these memories that now filled her head while she prayed; they helped keep her mind off the still unresolved issue of whether she and David should tell Ron who is real father was. She couldn't escape it, though; Ron kept popping up in her thoughts. She remembered when her dad had shared his plan with the rest of the family to remain in his home, but with Chris and David living with him. No one had been more thrilled than Ron.

Chris could still vividly see them all at the camp, eating the remains of casseroles and salads the townsfolk had brought to the house during her mom's calling hours.

Ron had exclaimed, "I get to live with Grandpa? Yeah!"

Chris often had told others that the reason her dad was doing so well, as the years passed, was because Ron was around. Her father was happy and healthy, and Ron thrived in his grandfather's presence. David's relationship with Ron, however, was less than perfect. From time to time, Chris sensed a tension between them. She never expressed her concern to David, though, lest he say, "He's not my son!"

Fortunately her fears were unfounded. Chris never heard those words from David. He interacted with Ron, attended his practices and plays, drove him to Little League, and bandaged his scraped knees. Even so, Chris was aware that his behavior toward Ron stood in contrast to how he treated Greg. She was aware of a certain lack of affection; when Ron achieved on the field or in the classroom, David wasn't as kind and supportive as he had been with Greg.

Chris's father had taken a genuine interest in Ron since the time of his birth. At the age of seventy-two, Hal Wright was slowing down, and Chris couldn't be sure her father still had the energy or desire to crawl out of bed each day to go off to the mill. Yet he was determined to keep doing it. Perhaps his rising early and having breakfast with Ron was his motivation.

Maybe this is why her dad had asked Chris, long before her mother had died, how she and David would feel about moving back to Cooperstown. It became apparent her father wanted to stay in his home. Plus he knew with Chris there he'd be taken care of. Chris prayed that Diane and Hal, Jr., would be content with their father's proposal.

"Well for me," Hal, Jr., had said, "it'll be good to have my big sister back in town. Maybe we could even get Ron a part-time job at the mill when he's old enough."

"Oh, wow! Really? Can I?" Ron joyfully asked.

David sternly added, "We'll see, Ron, how your schoolwork goes and if you have the time. That's still a few years away."

Chris heard a vibrating hum, and as she opened her eyes, she spotted a hummingbird working its way from petunia to petunia in the basket of flowers that hung nearby. Looking out from the front porch, she delighted at the Technicolor view of lush green lawns, mature trees, manicured shrubbery, and vibrant flowers.

What a wise decision it was for us to relocate here, she thought. *It's hard to believe it's been twenty-two years already. Thanks, Dad, for urging us to return home.*

Her mind raced back to the time when her dad had gathered his family around the dining room table. She recalled that she was unsure how her siblings would react and wanted to be prepared. She had put together a little speech that she had consigned to memory and never quite forgot.

"As you've heard Dad share," she began, "he wants to stay in the family home. We all love the place. I know I love it as much as Diane and Hal, who also grew up there. If this arrangement that Dad's proposing would work for everyone, I think David and I could return to Cooperstown, bring our family, and be here for

Dad. Greg's now at SU, and DeEtte starts college this year. Ron's only eleven and says he'd be happy to live with Grandpa and be near the Baseball Hall of Fame. So our kids seem to be on board. I just need to know that you, Hal and Diane, are comfortable with this. David and I hope we can move in by Thanksgiving so there'll be no change in where you'll come for your turkey dinner."

Chris, only forty-six at the time, had paused and thought, *Do I sound like the new mother barking out the new order of things?*

There was a moment of waiting. Looking straight at Chris, Hal, Jr., was the first to speak. "I can't believe we'll be neighbors. I think it's great. And Dad, you'll still be at the house, where all of Cooperstown expects to find you. It sounds perfect."

Chris glanced around the table, anxious for any reaction. Seven grandchildren sat quietly interspersed among the adults. They ranged in age from nine years old to twenty, and as if they'd been instructed, they sat attentive, listening to this very adult conversation for the past fifteen minutes. Everyone appeared privileged to have been invited to share in Grandpa Wright's wishes for himself and his children. Whether a grandchild, step-grandchild, son, or daughter-in-law, they all loved and had a deep respect for Hal Wright, Sr., whose heart was as big as the outdoors.

He had listened to his son with admiration in his eyes as he awaited Diane, who shared her thoughts as she glanced around the table. "I've been away from home over ten years," she said. "And although I love the house I grew up in, John and I have really made our home in the Hamptons. I feel rather selfish, though. I haven't been there to help out at the mill or to help Chris with Dad. If Chris and David are willing to move back with their family, I think it is a great idea."

"Diane, you're my daughter, and you're as much a part of this family as everyone else. Please don't feel guilty that you don't live closer. You and John have made a very good life for yourselves.

I'm just happy that Chris and David are willing to relocate. So please don't feel badly," her father offered.

Should I have been surprised at how loving and cordial everyone was? Chris thought now. Her mother had frequently said to her, "You can get through anything, Christine, if there's enough love."

Chris rose out of her rocker a bit unsteadily and, placing her hands on the railing, thought, *That's it! David and I have to believe Ron loves us enough to be able to hear this news and that he'll still love us after we've told him.*

CHAPTER 14

It had been a week since Chris and David had returned from their weeklong stay at camp. Clothes had been washed and put away, the refrigerator restocked, the house cleaned. She and David were beginning to think of the next time they'd be traveling north to camp. They already had decided on Labor Day weekend but thought they might slip in a Sunday-through-Tuesday trip in the meantime.

Now they were reading magazines on the back deck, and drinking late-morning cups of coffee, when the phone rang. David had brought the phone out with him earlier and now answered it.

"Chris, it's for you," he said, handing her the phone.

"Hello," Chris spoke into the receiver.

"Chris, this is Carl Taylor."

In a split second, fifty-some years passed before her eyes. When had she last heard this voice? December 1957.

She wasn't surprised that it was Carl. Since she had read Fred's letter, she knew that sooner or later he would call. In contrast she felt that David was hoping beyond all hope that the call never would come.

Before responding, Chris mouthed, "It's Carl" to David.

Only a second or two had passed, and Chris hadn't responded. She thought it intriguing that a voice she hadn't heard in more than fifty years would have this familiarity. He was articulate and his tone was warm and pleasant, just as she had remembered.

Her failure to respond prompted Carl. "Chris, did you receive a letter from my father?"

She drew in a deep breath, Vivaldi's *Four Seasons* floated from the kitchen radio. She needed to relax. She needed to listen to Carl. "Yes, I did. I received it a week ago. We had been up at camp, and it was waiting for me when we returned."

"I received my letter last week too," Carl said. "It's taken me and my wife a bit of time to sort all this out. I had no idea, Chris. You and my father? I have a brother?"

Carl abruptly ended his questioning, for which Chris was grateful. She wondered how many more questions were forthcoming. With the intervening time between receiving the letter and this phone call, she wondered why she hadn't thought about the potential conversation. She hadn't given thought to what she might say if Carl were to inquire about her relationship with his father. She hesitated.

Carl again interrupted the silence. "How are you, Chris?"

Perhaps it was his tone or her flashback to happier days, but she responded warmly. "Oh, Carl, I'm fine. But in your dad's letter, he explained that you aren't so well."

"I'm not sure how much he explained to you," Carl said, "but I really need your help. Is it possible we could meet soon so I could better explain my situation?"

Chris looked at David, whose eyes were fixed on hers. She responded, "Carl, can I get back to you? My husband David and I need to talk this over. You need to know that our son Ron has no idea that your father is also his. I haven't seen your father or had any contact with him in thirty-four years, and our son believes David is his father. He knows nothing about your dad, and right now David and I need to think about this."

Carl's voice was strong and resolute. "You know, Chris, your son's bone marrow could save my life."

She heard desperation in this voice and felt he was begging for her to make a decision right then; she heard it in his voice.

"I'm aware that you need some answers, Carl. But please give us some time."

"That's the one thing I don't have a lot of, Chris—time."

"Carl, give me your phone number, and let me call you back after David and I have sorted through all of this," Chris offered. "We'll try to do everything we can to help."

She grabbed a pen from the table and wrote quickly as Carl gave her his home and cell phone numbers. She even took down his e-mail address; she wrote everything on the back cover of a *Time* magazine.

"All right, Chris. I hope to hear from you soon. Bye for now."

Chris placed the phone back down then looked across the table at David. He said nothing, but having heard only one side of the conversation, he waited for Chris to fill him in on the details.

"He wants to meet with me soon," she said. "It's obvious he sees Ron as someone who can possibly save his life. What are we going to do?" Chris was beside herself, struggling with Fred's letter, Carl's request, and David's negative attitude toward the whole situation.

They spoke about it throughout the day. When it grew dark, they withdrew from the back deck and ascended the staircase. As they sat on the loveseat in their bedroom, small snifters of brandy in hand, they each shared their concerns about the decision they were about to make. They talked about their family, each repeating memories from their thirty-plus years marriage, decisions made, promises kept.

"From the very beginning, I never meant to dump this in your lap," Chris said apologetically.

"You don't get it, do you? I took everything into account when I married you. I loved and wanted you and everything you would bring to this marriage. I wouldn't have changed anything, Chris."

She put her head on David's shoulder as he reached for her hand.

Over the years they had experienced joys and sorrows, as all families do. Perhaps revisiting their memories would give them the hope that, as they moved forward, they could survive anything.

David rose and paced the floor, much like an expectant father. If they told Ron the truth, would it cause an irreparable breach between him and his son—a relationship that had grown and matured and strengthened over the past twenty years?

In the end they decided that Chris should call Carl the next day and plan to meet him. They didn't have all the answers, but Carl might offer some.

There still lingered the nagging question of when and how to tell Ron.

"I've been giving this a lot of thought," David said. "I've prayed about it too. Ron is a priest. If he can't forgive us for keeping the truth from him all these years, who can? I've got to believe, like you said last week, that everything will work out."

Taking David's hand in hers, Chris said, "Oh, I hope so."

"Not to worry," David said two days later, as Chris prepared to make the drive to meet Carl. "I checked the Internet for Nancy's Diner in Sherburne and programmed it into the GPS while you were showering. You're all set."

"Right," murmured Chris. "All set." *I wish.*

She was worried. Yet in a strange way, she was looking forward to this encounter after all these years of separation, wondering how it would play out. She knew this was part of the process—the anticipation.

It had only taken a day, after Carl's call, for David and Chris to come to some decisions—talking things over, thinking about how they could share this news with Ron.

Chris had called Carl. He was elated to hear her voice, especially when she said she'd be happy to meet with him. He had suggested coffee the next day, halfway between their homes.

David mentioned that it would take Chris forty-five minutes to make the drive. She departed at exactly nine fifteen. She neither wanted to sit waiting for Carl nor arrive late.

She pulled into a parking place along the main street of Sherburne, New York, with two minutes to spare. Even on this busy morning, the traffic had moved along quickly, making for a hassle-free trip.

Chris had dressed in a cap-sleeve, green, summer print dress that fit her size-ten frame well. She had considered high heels but opted for a pair of dressy sandals. She was pleased with her healthy-looking tan, which had been greatly enhanced after a week at camp.

As she walked along the sidewalk, she drew her hand to her cheek. She knew her face was flushed, and she just hoped it wasn't too evident. *I can't let that worry me now*, she decided as she walked up the two front steps of Nancy's, a red-shingled diner. She thought of the shoulder-length blonde hair she'd had when she and Carl last saw each other. It had been fifteen years since she had opted for a shorter over-the-ear style that was easier to manage and was now kept blonde with help. She was curious to know whether he'd recognize her. During their phone conversation, she hadn't thought to ask if she should wear a distinguishing item that would identify her.

As she entered through the screened door, Carl rose from a booth. The familiar smell of frying bacon filled the air. About half the booths along the front windows were occupied with young and old, enjoying everything from pancakes to omelets. Two old gents wearing ball caps sat on stools at the counter, engaged in a heated discussion.

As Chris walked to where Carl stood waiting, her first impression was how wonderful he looked. He was perhaps a few inches taller than she remembered, had a bit less brown hair, and was still slender, much like he had been in 1957. In contrast to her tan, he was very pale, and immediately she realized, *Of course. He's in cancer treatment—no sun tanning for him.*

Beaming with a smile, she headed over to him. His open and welcoming arms greeted her, and they stood for a few moments in a warm embrace, silent.

Drawing back and holding her at the elbows, Carl looked directly into her eyes. "Chris, you look fantastic."

"Thank you, Carl. So do you."

Almost simultaneously they both said, "Perhaps we should sit down."

Although Chris was thinking it, Carl said, "Didn't we say that once on your raft? How many years ago was that?"

Chris ordered coffee as the waitress came around to warm up Carl's cup, and he added an order of English muffins with jam to share.

"I have a million questions," he said. "Would you mind?"

"Not at all, Carl."

"I need to know how you and my dad got together. He didn't share any details in my letter, just that you two had reconnected on Seventh Lake, and your pregnancy was a result of that. I've got to tell you, Chris, when I read his letter, I couldn't believe it."

Chris whispered, "I am so sorry."

Carl continued, "First, to realize that he had sexual relations with you that resulted in a pregnancy and somewhere out there I had a half-brother...well, I was bowled over. I mean, I still think of you as a teenager and to now realize that my father made love to you... It's almost beyond belief. Why?"

Carl's question floated in the air. Chris was trying hard not to stare at Carl as he spoke. She was grateful Fred hadn't said any more than was necessary in explaining the incident, because she wasn't going to share the details either.

The night before, she had lain in bed thinking about this reunion and wondering how she would talk about the intimacy.

Initially she thought she would share with Carl how his father had forced himself on her. She quickly rejected that line of thinking, not only because she didn't want to present Carl with that image of his dad, but also, to a greater extent, when she finally came to her senses in the last forty-eight hours about what had really happened those thirty-plus years ago, she thought she best share a more accurate representation of the actual events. She was still very concerned, however, about what Carl would think of her. She didn't want to come across as a hussy who had seduced his father.

Chris began, "I was out canoeing, and suddenly a severe thunder and lightning storm came up. Your dad hollered at me to get off the lake. He didn't recognize me. Over coffee I told him who I was and that I had hated him since he had broken us up all those years ago with his phone call. He apologized, said he was sorry. What could I say? It had been almost twenty years."

She paused momentarily as she envisioned that first encounter with Fred Taylor, and then said to Carl, "I told him I forgave him. We had coffee again the next morning, and he invited me to dinner at his rental cottage. He said your mom was at a teaching conference and wouldn't arrive at the camp until the end of the week. He was being nice. I canoed over to his camp that night. He cooked dinner and gave me a couple of pretty stiff drinks—scotch. I probably should have known better. Then he poured wine to go with the steaks."

Chris knew she had to tell Carl what happened next. She was embarrassed and looked down at his cup of coffee. She just couldn't make eye contact when she said, "He came on to me, Carl. I succumbed to his charm and advances. We made love."

She couldn't believe what she had just said to Carl. *I made love with your father,* she thought. She felt awkward but continued, "I left when he fell asleep, and I never saw him again."

She conveniently left off any mention of his father's pursuit of her in the days that followed. Only now, as she glanced up at

Carl, did Chris realize he hadn't taken his eyes off her. She looked intently at him, realizing how difficult these words were for him to hear.

Across the table sat her first love; his eyes looked sad. Chris saw a man who could be dying. Having just revealed the details of her tryst with Carl's father, she wondered, *Have I added yet another burden for him to carry?*

She had agonized over the words to explain what happened. She wanted to get it over in the fastest and simplest way possible. She came to the realization that she never had written down the details of that week in a journal or notebook and had discussed the event only with David and Father Jim; even then it had been without great detail or elaboration—only what was absolutely necessary.

As she responded to a question Carl asked regarding her decision to give birth to his father's child, she felt a sudden twinge in her stomach. Maybe it was the result of telling her story for the first time in thirty-four years, or a physical reaction to her second cup of regular coffee, which she rarely drank these days.

She excused herself to the ladies' room—none too soon, as she quickly moved into a stall and bent over the toilet. Her stomach wrenched, and she vomited what seemed to be everything she had consumed over the last twenty-four hours. She heaved, wondering how long her sickness would last.

When it was over, she leaned against the metal stall door to steady herself.

Was I more stressed out about this encounter than I thought? My body must be telling me I've kept too much inside for too long.

She washed up quickly, wishing she had some mouthwash. She resorted to rinsing her mouth with a bit of soap and water.

On her way to her seat, she caught the eye of the waitress and, after calling her over, ordered a ginger ale, hoping it might settle her stomach.

Carl noticed that she was flushed. "Are you all right?" he asked. "I'll be fine."

"So, Chris, going back to your time at camp with my dad, was that it?"

"It was, Carl. I avoided him. I didn't canoe his way for the rest of the week. I went hiking and visited friends. I returned home and tried to forget about it until I found out I was pregnant."

For the next fifteen minutes, Chris spoke about David and his acceptance of the child she had conceived out of wedlock. She talked briefly of her stepchildren, DeEtte and Greg, and Greg's premature death while serving his country.

Carl, playing with his silverware, took in all the revelations Chris was recounting. He expressed gratitude that under the circumstances she was willing to meet with him.

Now it was Chris's turn to urge Carl to talk about his life. "Can you fill me in on your life since we broke up?" she asked, smiling and thinking of all the years that had passed since their last conversation.

She was both relieved and saddened when he talked about the events that had led to his dad's fateful call to her that December in 1957.

"Believe me, Chris. It was the last thing I wanted, but my father made the decision. Thinking back on that era, I wasn't about to disobey my dad, who was going to be paying my way through college after graduation. He asked me to have no more contact with you, and I did as told. I'm sorry if I hurt you by never reaching out to you again."

"It's in the past, Carl. Let's let it be."

Carl described his journey from being a senior in high school to now being a retired CPA, his happy marriage, his daughters and grandchildren, and the memorable vacations they'd taken throughout the years. He didn't shy away from discussing some of his joys and disappointments. Chris listened intently to every word and was happy to see a smile on Carl's face. At times his vivid descriptions and detail caused her to feel she had shared in his life's adventures.

"And then a few months ago, I was diagnosed with leukemia," Carl said, "and now I need a bone marrow transplant. My dad wanted to be tested, but the doctors thought he was too old and frail to even be considered. I remember some of the conversations we had this year on Father's Day. He wasn't saying it directly, but I could detect that he knew his time was short. And he was so concerned about my health needs. Honestly, Chris, he would have done anything to make sure I recovered from this cancer. It must have been soon after that he decided to let both of us know what he hoped Ron might do to help me."

Carl took a deep breath and a sip of his coffee, then continued, "When I read my dad's letter, I was in shock. Never in my wildest imagination could I have thought up anything like this. It was like a bad dream. I was so angry at my father...and at you."

"I'm truly sorry for my actions so long ago, Carl. You probably hate me." She sensed Carl was, in fact, seeing her far differently than he had when she was fifteen years old

He didn't respond to her last statement but asked, "Do you think there's a possibility of your asking your son if he'd be tested to see if he's a match?"

Chris's nerves were showing, as her fingers seemed to be playing out a very fast melody on the tabletop. She stopped and looked at Carl. "You need to know that Ron doesn't know that your father is also his. Since Ron was born, David has been his father. No one needed to know any different," Chris told him. "Be assured—I'm going to do whatever I can to make sure you're around for many years to come. But first I have to sit down with my son, who, by the way, is a priest. I'm not sure if your father added that in his letter. Isn't that fascinating, Carl? Your father once put an end to your involvement with a Catholic girl and now has a son who's a priest."

"It's more than fascinating, Chris. For me it's truly a Godsend."

Chris sipped her ginger ale. Her stomach felt better as she sensed the tension between them had been somewhat relieved.

Carl slid a piece of paper across the table. "I'm under the care of a great doctor in Syracuse. I have his name and number listed here, as well as my home address, phone numbers, and e-mail. I wanted to be sure you could reach me day or night at home or by cell. Could you please stay in touch and let me know what's happening? If Ron needs more information, or if he decides to help, he can simply call my doctor."

When they rose from the table, the large round clock on wall read ten after eleven. Carl paid the check at the cash register, where the two old gents were still discussing seemingly pressing matters.

As they stepped outside into a glorious sunny day, Carl walked Chris to her car. The difficulty in saying good-bye became obvious to both. They gave each other a quick hug. Chris reassured him that she hoped to communicate with him soon and that perhaps somewhere along the way he and his wife and David and she might get together.

"That would be great!" Carl said. "If anyone can make it happen, I know you can."

"Bye for now," Chris offered, as she made her way to the driver's side of the vehicle.

Before she turned the key in the ignition, she took out her cell phone from her purse. She needed to call David and fill him in on every detail of their meeting before she went anywhere.

"David," she said, "I'm going to call Ron right now to see if and when we can get together. Do you want to be with me when I tell him? If he's free right now, I could drive to St. Anne's and talk to him. What do you think?"

"This can't go well," David said. "I guess I'd rather wait and see how he reacts. If you can handle it, have at it."

Chris always had known this secret had been of her making and at this moment took full responsibility. "You're right. It isn't going to be pretty, but the truth has got to finally come out. Would there ever be a better time than the present?"

After Chris got off the phone with David, she made the quick call to Ron. He seemed receptive but curious.

"Mom, what's so important? Has something happened?"

"As a matter of fact, something has, Ron. I need to sit down with you," Chris said with a sense of urgency.

"OK. Come to the rectory. We can have lunch and talk."

As soon as her call to Ron was complete, she redialed David and told him she was on her way to see their son. She took a deep breath. This wasn't going to be easy.

CHAPTER 15

It took Chris almost an hour to reach St. Anne's Church. Thoughts of Ron's recent stay with them at camp filled her head. It was that first night after Ron had celebrated Mass when he planned to prepare grilled chicken for dinner. Chris could still see him as he scampered up and down the front steps, tending first to starting the charcoal and later to the chicken. In the meantime he joined his mother and father, who were enjoying pre-dinner cocktails.

Perhaps it was something to do with his saying Mass—Chris couldn't quite remember—but something prompted Ron to recount that his announcement about wanting to be a priest had occurred at camp sixteen years earlier.

Immediately Chris had said, "How well we remember that August when you gave your dad and me a little bit of anxiety."

"Really? I always thought you were happy for me."

"It wasn't a matter of being happy for you," Chris told him. "It was all those plans we had envisioned for you that went quickly down the drain."

As Chris sipped her Manhattan and bit into a piece of cheese, she asked David, who looked very relaxed, "How vividly do you remember that week when Ron shared his thoughts about becoming a priest?"

"Oh, very well. Don't you remember after Greg's death how we both thought that it would now probably be Ron who would follow your brother's lead, go to work at the mill, and run the company one day?"

After grabbing another can of beer, Ron sat down on the porch railing, all ears.

"As best as I can recall, Ron," Chris said, "it was our traditional week at camp. It was the third summer you had worked for the lumber company, and your Uncle Hal, as he did each year, said you could have the week off to go to camp with us. Actually his exact words were, 'Take a swim for me.' You took a great interest in your work during those years, working with your uncle."

"You're right. I did," interjected Ron. "What I loved most was getting up in the morning with Grandpa Wright, enjoying breakfast together, and then walking the quarter-mile to the mill. Some of the best history lessons I ever got I learned alongside Grandpa."

Chris wondered whether Ron's close relationship with his grandfather made up for the strained one between Ron and David in the years immediately following Greg's death. She also was grateful for the opportunity Ron had during his teen years to value and appreciate his grandfather.

Harold Wright was described by some as a rough, tough, no-nonsense guy. He was all that and more—a man who would give you the shirt off his back, literally. The townsfolk knew him not just as a local businessman who served his community well, but also as a quiet man who went out of his way to assist those in need. This is what Ron had witnessed, what he had been exposed to day in and day out. And just as his grandfather had become his role model, Ron gave his grandfather good reason so stay healthy and alive.

On more than one occasion, Chris's father had come to Ron's defense when David had found fault with his shoveling or mowing. Ron, however, could do no wrong in his granddad's eyes.

Chris had taken note of the subtle changes right after Greg's death, understanding that his tragic passing was difficult for David. His firstborn son was gone forever. David had filled his days at work writing and helping manage the newspaper, but when evenings and weekends came, he seemed to take out his frustrations on Ron. He loved him—Chris never questioned that—but during those first few years, Chris worked hard at trying to rationalize this aspect of David's grief.

Chris glanced at the clock on the dash of the car. She was making excellent time over a road she couldn't remember ever being upon. The countryside was right out of an "I Love New York" poster—green, lush, tranquil, and dotted here and there with a herd of Holstein cattle.

She returned to her thoughts of camp and Ron's recollections about wanting to become a priest.

"Ron, I remember that Grandpa Wright was here with us, and you spent a lot of time with him out in the rowboat fishing," Chris had told him. "I think there were also a couple of maintenance projects he wanted to do, and I took pictures while you helped him out."

David had noted, "Your mom's right, Ron. You worked well with your granddad, and it seemed natural for you to follow in his footsteps. And then, halfway through that week, as we sat at the table, you announced that you were thinking about the priesthood. It came as a bolt out of the blue."

Chris interjected, "I know in those first few moments after you dropped your bomb, I thought back on the fact that you probably had done all the things young men do who feel they have a religious vocation. You had been active at St. Mary's as an altar boy and then president of the CYO, but at that time, we had no idea that you had stayed in touch with Father Jim. We didn't know that once you had started driving you were making regular trips to see him. You really kept us in the dark. I mean, let's remember, you had a steady girlfriend, you dated, and you enjoyed parties. Missy was at our house all the time and stayed for dinner at least once a week. You didn't seem to be sending any messages, at least that I was picking up on, that you were thinking of becoming a priest."

Perhaps the recollections David and I spoke of at camp might bring per-
spective and better understanding to Ron as he struggles with his vocation
now, Chris hoped, as she made the drive to St. Anne's.

She knew Ron had shared and discussed much of his decision-
making that summer of 1994 when he had broken the news.

"Do you remember Grandpa's reaction?" Ron had asked her.
"How he grabbed me and put those big hands of his around me
and said, 'I'm so happy for you, my boy.' He was the one I hadn't
really thought about when I decided to share my news, and I
couldn't have planned or expected his reaction."

For the next half-hour, the conversation danced around the
porch, Ron taking the lead and Chris following. Then David broke
in, adding details and correcting others.

Chris finally said, "You have to remember, Ron, that the family business has played a big role in all of our lives. Your dad and I
had seen you in action at the mill. You had a great work ethic. You
did your job well and looked for additional things to do. I came to
believe that you were in the queue to join the firm after college."

By the mid-1990s, Chris believed the future of the company was
in good hands. Ron was close to his cousin Eric, his Uncle Hal's
youngest son, who would begin his freshman year at Hamilton.
Chris also knew Eric wanted to be part of the company, especially
now that his older brother Hal, III, had graduated from Colgate
and had been accepted into medical school.

The idea of Chris's nephew becoming a doctor was a powerful
statement about not only the hopes and dreams of a new genera-
tion but also its new opportunities.

"It is ironic, isn't it, thinking back on our discussions in the
nineties, that we didn't give thought to the fact that it would be
your cousin Carol who today would be in line to succeed her father
as company president?"

"You're right, Mom. We all just need to follow our heart. I'd
been giving a lot of thought to becoming a priest, even though

I had a lot going on in my life. Believe it or not, I shared my thoughts with Missy, and she often went to church with me on Saturday afternoons to sit and pray at St. Mary's. She was happy for me, which took a big weight off my shoulders. I didn't want to hurt anyone with my decision." Ron paused in his recollections as he leaned against the newel post at the top of the porch steps.

Momentarily Chris now recalled her father standing in that same spot on his last visit to camp, just two weeks after 9/11. Hal Wright, Sr., had asked his daughter if she could take a day off from work so the two of them could spend a day together. With his health deteriorating, Chris sensed this might be his last trip.

The trees were at their peak; the profusion of reds, yellows, and oranges creating the perfect picture for the cover of a September issue of Adirondack Life. Was it any wonder photographers flocked to the region this time of year? She could hear her father's words—*Isn't it beautiful, Chris? You really have to see it with your own eyes. Pictures don't do it justice. Mountain after mountain. So lovely.*

When they had arrived at camp, Chris had helped him out of his car, which he still owned and maintained but had given up driving. She made sure he had his cane in hand.

"Let's walk around to the dock before we go in," he urged. As they slowly meandered and finally stood on the dock, he said, "I'm going to miss it. I hope God gives me this view from heaven. I know you're going to continue to take great care of Lake Wrights, Chris, so that it'll be in good hands for generations to come."

"Dad, do you want to sit on the front porch for a bit?"

Hal didn't speak but simply turned and, grabbing his daughter's arm, walked the forty feet to the front steps. He let go of her arm as he made his way up, then grabbed hold of the newel post at the top and clung to it.

"Chris, did I ever tell you how we made these posts when the camp was built?"

Chris had heard the story many, many times but said, "Tell me again, Dad."

Hal explained how, in 1950, his brothers, a couple of friends and he had cut and trimmed two pine trees to eight feet, hauled them back to the mill and trimmed them up. Then they had placed them on a lathe and turned them to produce the matching newel posts that had held up the front porch beam and roof for the past sixty years. "They're as beautiful today as they were then, holding everything up and in place. They sure have stood the test of time, although there's a split here in the wood."

Chris often recalled her dad's words about that flawed newel post. It was so like her family—strong, stable, and resilient. Yet when you got up close, you might see the cracks.

Again Chris was brought back to the present, wishing she had thought to bring along a bottle of water. She was thirsty. Mozart played softly on the public radio station as she returned to her ongoing replay of treasured moments.

What a great last memory of my dad to have, thought Chris, as she refocused her thoughts, trying not to forget any of Ron's story.

"I don't know if I ever shared with you what happened to me that week that was so significant to my decision," Ron had said that day on the porch at camp. "I went out in the canoe, paddling down the back side of the lake, and everything seemed perfect. The temperature was in the low eighties, the sky was blue, and the lake was mirror-like. I could see to the bottom, and I had my fishing pole in hand. I'd been casting and watching my bobber for a half-hour or so. I'd caught a few perch. I'd used my net to bring one of them into the boat. It was then that I had a feeling come over me, as if God were speaking directly to me. At that moment the words of Matthew's Gospel hit me, where Jesus says to Simon and Andrew, 'Come after me, and I will make you fishers of men.' Then they left their nets and followed him. It seemed that everything I'd been thinking and praying about for so long suddenly made sense, and I simply said, 'Yes!' I was overwhelmed that I had made the decision. I never looked back and never had any doubts, second thoughts, or reservations. At that moment I couldn't have been happier. And, as they say, the rest is history."

It was thoughts about Ron's history—his relationships, his growing-up years, his eight years in the priesthood—that now prompted Chris to ask herself, *Will all those good memories outweigh the burden I'm about to lay on him?*

She'd find out soon enough. She parked her car in front of the rectory, which was made of red brick, just like church next door. Like many of the other churches in the city, St. Anne's possessed beautiful stained-glass windows, murals on the walls, and a choir loft that held a magnificent organ. Ron had been assigned here seven years ago, and Chris and David frequently drove to Utica to be present for Mass.

At the front door of the rectory, Ron greeted his mother with a warm embrace then showed her into the stately dining room. He too had picked up some sun during their week at camp, and Chris realized he must have gotten a haircut since his return. He looked clean-cut, almost like a young executive, wearing a short-sleeve blue dress shirt and khaki pants.

The large rectangular table in the center of the room had been spread with a yellow tablecloth and matching napkins. The cloth, on which Ron had set out a pitcher of iced tea and tuna salad sandwiches, lent an air of brightness and warmth to the room.

As Ron sat down in the chair at the head of the table, his back to a bank of windows, he asked, "What's up, Mom?"

Chris found Ron's curiosity not unusual. How many times in his life had she left him hanging as he waited for more information? This wasn't the first time, and she was sure it wouldn't be the last.

"Ron, before I explain everything to you, I want you to read a letter. Two weeks ago at camp, when I read the obituary of Fred Taylor, you had a lot of questions. This will explain some things.

She reached into her purse, took the letter from the envelope, and handed it to Ron.

She poured herself a tall glass of iced tea and drank. She needed to quench her thirst.

Ron read the letter slowly, never lifting his eyes from the written words. It took him three minutes to read. When he finished, rather than hand it back to his mother, he placed it on the table next to his plate. Only now did he lift his hazel eyes and stare directly into his mother's. He said nothing, nor did Chris. He threw his napkin down on the table, stood up, and walked to the windows, where he drew back the curtain, as if to see something more clearly.

Chris waited patiently. Finally Ron turned and walked to the back of his chair, over which he dangled his arms. "Does Dad know I'm not his son?"

"Yes, Ron. When I found I was pregnant in September of nineteen seventy-six, your dad and I were dating. He'd had a vasectomy several years before. He knew I wanted a baby of my own, and it was one of the reasons I'd been reluctant to marry him. I was only thirty-four and so wanted a child of my own. Your dad felt, in many ways, that the fact that I was pregnant solved the problem. I could have this baby. Your father was fully aware that I never would see the man who had fathered you again. Your dad said we could be married, and when the baby came seven months later, people would just assume I'd gotten pregnant before the wedding. Isn't that what you've assumed? Your father has kept my secret all these years."

Ron hung on every word his mother shared. Chris noticed the wet armpits of his shirt. She had been dabbing her own neck with her napkin.

"I went to confession with Father Jim as soon as I returned from camp that August," Chris said. "I felt terrible. I knew I had sinned but kept telling myself it really wasn't my fault, that I had been seduced. It only happened once, Ron. When I found out I was pregnant, I told Father Jim what your father's and my plans were and asked that he keep our secret. He's known the truth all these years."

Chris rose from her seat and walked to a sideboard, above which hung the familiar painting *The Road to Emmaus*. She appeared to be examining it, looking for something hidden. Slowly she turned back to Ron, who remained slumped over his chair.

"When you entered the priesthood, Father Jim begged me to finally share the truth with you, but frankly, Ron, I've always felt so guilty about what happened. I didn't want you to know how sinful your mother had been."

Chris poured herself some more iced tea and took a swallow. She wanted to walk over and throw her arms around her son. She thought better of it, however, and stood near her chair and continued, "The letter you just read was waiting for me when we arrived home from camp. A couple of days ago, Carl called, and we just met for coffee. He explained his need for a bone marrow transplant and requested that I ask you about it. I told him I'd never told you the truth about your father. I needed to do that first. I'm so sorry, Ron, that I couldn't be honest with you until now. I truly am."

Chris saw the tears welling up in Ron's eyes. He took a handkerchief from his pocket and blew his nose. Clearing his throat, he said, "Mom, I think you'd better leave. I love you, but I need to take some time alone and pray about this. You've just told me that the father I've known for the past thirty-three years isn't my father—and a half-brother I didn't know I had needs my bone marrow. You've got to admit, Mom, that it's a lot to drop on a guy. At some point over the years—when I became an adult—why didn't you tell me? Why have you let me be part of this lie all this time?"

Ron was keeping the volume of his voice at a level below screaming, but Chris heard the anger and disappointment in his voice, his obvious outrage at hearing this news.

She placed her napkin on her plate and, wishing to honor her son's request, made her way out of the dining room. Tears fell down her cheeks and spotted her dress as she walked through the hallway and out the front door. She didn't look back.

CHAPTER 16

As Chris drove east on Route 5, she felt numb. Perhaps, more than anything, she was angry with herself. She called David. Her palms were sweaty. "I've just left Ron," she said in a disappointing tone.

"How did it go?"

"Not well. I'll share everything with you when I get home."

Spontaneously she pulled her car over to the curb and got out. There was a small park to her right that was large enough to accommodate a swing set and ball field. Tall maples shaded a walkway, where she found a bench.

If Chris had learned anything in her years of praying—and her children certainly had come to understand her need and desire for daily meditation—it was the power of something outside of oneself. She knew Ron had a deep spirituality and trusted he would draw on that faith over the next few days. She decided to leave him alone and let him sort things out for himself with the help of a higher power.

Ron had been an unexpected gift. After her ten-year marriage to Mike, she was almost positive she'd never have the experience of a pregnancy, no opportunity to bring a child into the world. She was bewildered when her doctor had told her she going to have a baby. She stood there in disbelief. After so many years of waiting and wanting, she now was expecting a baby as a result of her brief sexual encounter with a married man.

Nevertheless she was pregnant and thrilled about it. But she was likewise terrified by the reality of the situation and how she would deal with it personally, as well as how she would tell David and her folks.

Just a week before, when she, though uncertain she was pregnant, had accepted David's marriage proposal, she wondered how she would share the story of her time at camp, and her encounter with Fred Taylor, if a pregnancy was confirmed. Would David call off the engagement? She couldn't be sure. All she could think about at the time was Kathy Yates, her friend Linda's sister, and the talk that went on in whispered conversations after her return to school. Chris envisioned comments about her behind closed doors—comments of a grown woman having had sex and giving birth to a child out of wedlock.

When she became a wife and stepmother in one day's time, she had no idea how the attitudes and behavior of friends and associates would change with regard to her. She instantly became part of a married community she never had experienced, even when she had been Mike's wife.

Before she and David had announced to the world their planned child, which they delayed until Thanksgiving that year, Chris found herself a stepmother to a nine-year-old and a seven-year-old. Suddenly she was going to PTA meetings and school plays and making arrangements for dance lessons and soccer practice.

She quickly realized that the independent, single life she'd come to know had vanished. She was a wife and mother and, almost overnight, discovered something about herself. It was no longer all about Chris; there were other responsibilities in her life. And she grew to love everything about her new environment, home, and social status.

Nothing, however, had prepared her for the feelings she had experienced when Ron was born. Within days of his birth, she broke down in tears as she gazed at him in his crib.

Thank you, Lord, for this gift, she had prayed. Chris knew what it was to love and be loved; all of her life she had been surrounded by it. She discovered that having a child added a new and unexpected dimension of love. She was consumed by the desire to give love, to nurture, and to protect this precious baby boy God had given her.

Now two young boys skated by on their boards, distracting Chris from her thoughts. *What is Ron thinking?* she wondered.

She was fairly certain that from the time Ron had entered his teenage years and discovered his birthday fell just seven months after his parents celebrated their anniversary, he had to wonder.

I'm assuming he always believed his father and I were intimate before we were married, and as a result, he was conceived, she thought. *He never asked us about it. I'm sure he didn't want to embarrass us or himself. Now he's learned that it wasn't David at all. He must hate us for not telling him the truth.*

She needed to get back on the road; David would be waiting for her.

Ten minutes into her journey, she realized she no longer was in possession of Fred's letter; it had remained on Ron's table. It was her only copy.

Why didn't I think to make a copy? she asked herself. She felt pretty secure that Ron wouldn't destroy it. She'd feel better, however, when it was back in her hands. *I've read the letter over and over. I'm sure Ron will too.*

She tried to relax; the air conditioning was making for a comfortable ride. She turned on Sirius radio and found the channel for Broadway show tunes. Angela Lansbury was singing, "If he walked into my life again…" from *Mame.* Chris lowered the volume.

She returned to her earlier thoughts about finding herself pregnant.

I remember how scared I was that Labor Day weekend at camp just weeks after the encounter with Fred. I had missed my period, and being as regular as I was, I felt pretty sure I was carrying Fred's child, but I hoped I was wrong. I remember sitting out at the end of the dock, wrapped in Grandma Wright's quilt, under a blanket of stars, after Greg and DeEtte had gone to sleep, and David joined me. He was so happy that all of us were together at Lake Wrights. He had heard me talk so much about going to camp over the years that he told me and my folks how privileged he felt to finally be there.

When he sat down next to me on the dock, he became very serious. He looked straight at me, took my right hand in his, and asked me to marry him. I was so lost in my own concerns about possibly being pregnant that I didn't hear him the first time, and he repeated, "Chris, will you marry me?"

I stared off across the lake, noticing the comforting lights reflecting from the camps and dancing across the water. And then David again said, "Chris, will you marry me?"

I thought about telling him the truth but figured that if I wasn't pregnant I might never have to share this dark secret. I'm just glad I finally had the good sense to almost shout, "Yes! Yes! Of course, I'll marry you. Oh, David, I know we can make this work."

It wasn't until a week later when my doctor confirmed the pregnancy that I had to face the fact and tell David. It was over dinner at our favorite trattoria in Utica that I finally opened up; I assume it was after a couple of glasses of wine that I shared what had transpired during that week at camp. I'll never forget the look on his face—the shocked look and his question to me, "What are you telling me, Chris? That you snuck off to camp and had an affair with a man while we were talking about marriage, and only now you're sharing this news with me?" He certainly wasn't expecting this revelation of a pregnancy. I was sure any plans of marriage were over. I was even twisting my engagement ring, which I'd only had for a few days, thinking I was going to have to give it back. But I answered all of his questions in as much detail as he wanted. I kept reiterating that it had happened once, that it was over, and I'd never see this man again.

Chris concentrated on making the turn from Route 5E to Route 28 South; she'd be home in thirty minutes. Her mind returned to David's initial shock and his request that she give him time to concentrate on the effect this would have on him and on their marriage and his kids, and whether he eventually would be able to accept this child as his own. Chris eagerly had told him to take as long as he needed; she loved him and his children and believed she would do her best to make a success of their marriage.

I told him I had talked at length with Father Jim, and if he wanted to also, that might help, she thought. *I remember the wait that week. David tried to avoid me as best he could at the newspaper office, and I kept my distance too. I didn't want to interfere. Five days later he suggested we meet with Father Jim. In retrospect I'm not sure David just wanted a witness, because he did most of the talking. He obviously had deliberated long and hard on the matter.*

That evening David seemed so understanding, so mature when he said, "The brief affair is behind you, Chris." *He went on to repeat many of the things I had shared earlier with him, including the fact that I was never going to see this man again.* "I know you want a baby," *he said.* "No one needs to know it isn't mine. Let's get married soon."

Chris remembered Father Jim's grin as David had asked so sincerely, one more time, for her to spend the rest of her life with him.

She often reflected on the hasty planning of the next month, with arrangements for an October wedding and the accompanying excitement of family and friends. Over the years she had embraced the words David had spoken to her the evening following their wedding. "It was perfect," he had said.

CHAPTER 17

As she pulled into the driveway, Chris found David mowing the back lawn. When he saw her, he shut off the mower and met her as she climbed out of the car. His clothes were soaked, his hair bedraggled.

"Give me the good and bad news," David said expectantly.

Chris didn't know where to begin. She laid her purse on the hood of the car, as if she needed her hands free to be able to tell her story.

"My meeting with Carl went well, but I don't know what happened. I had to excuse myself and got to the bathroom just in time before vomiting. I was able to get it together, and Carl and I were able to finally talk. Although I brought my letter along, I didn't offer to let him read it, and he didn't ask. It was the same with him. I have no idea how much his dad shared, but Carl didn't offer his letter to me either. Perhaps the letters are too personal to share. It's apparent that Carl really wants Ron to get tested to see if he's a match."

Chris grabbed her purse and headed to the back deck. David walked with her.

"My talk with Ron was far less productive. Interestingly the first question he asked me was if you knew. I shared how we had come to our decision before we were married. That may or may not have some effect on his thinking. He was very upset, to say the least," Chris continued. "He was nearly screaming, and I heard the anger in his voice. He kept questioning why we hadn't told him the truth. I kept telling him I was sorry, but that didn't seem to help. Finally he asked me to leave. He was sad; there were tears in his eyes. I felt so bad for him. He said he needed time to think about it. I can't blame him. I can't imagine how I'd react to hearing this kind of news."

"So I guess we just sit and wait. How concerned are you about what Ron might do?" David inquired.

Chris walked up and sat down in a chair on the deck as David stood on the steps, listening.

"You know, David, it's really out of my hands. I don't have a clue as to how Ron is internalizing this, what he'll do, how he'll react. He kept the letter from Fred. Perhaps rereading it might give him a better understanding of why I made the choices I did. I just know he'll do what's right. Don't you?"

David said nothing. Chris looked intently at him as he turned and sat down on the top step. Chris felt his pain and sensed he was physically exhausted and emotionally drained. David caught his bowed head in his hands as he slumped over.

They both sat in silence for several minutes.

David finally rose and, turning to Chris, offered, "Let's just pray that he doesn't keep us in suspense for too long. Do you want to take a walk and see what I did back here? I trimmed the bushes before I mowed. I think you'll like how they look. I'm almost done with the lawn."

She followed a sweaty David across the lush backyard. The rains and heat of summer had caused the garden to explode with blossoms, and the bushes had burst forth with a thick new growth. When Chris and her siblings were children, they had spent hours playing on the grass and in the shrubbery, and occasionally, with the help of their dad, had set up a badminton net or crochet wickets. The large flat surface here worked for both.

After she and David had moved here, he had suggested they build a wooden deck across the back of the house. Chris's dad was keen on the idea, suggesting he create a design for their approval. He even lent his guidance to the workmen from his company, who built the deck. Chris was amazed how quickly the project was completed, even the new sliding glass doors that were placed at the back of the dining room for easy access to the deck.

David and Chris hadn't realized what a restful place this would become for both of them. After a long day of work, having cocktails in the shade of your own backyard was a real gift. And the kids loved having their friends over for hot dogs and soda. Greg even had asked to construct a horseshoe pit. Although he had dug out the pits at the far end of the lawn, the deck offered a great view of them. David, especially, enjoyed when his sons took on DeEtte and Chris, pitching the horseshoes.

Over the years David had said the deck added a room to their house each summer, as they spent many daylight hours there. It was a true retreat and one where they could entertain friends and family. Chris hoped in the days to come it might offer her some respite, the solitude she needed.

She took a quick look around and told David he'd done a great job with the trimming. She wasn't making it up. He loved doing it, and he had not only an eye for sculpting but also a knack for dealing with the overgrown hedge.

"You go ahead and finish up here, David," she said. "I'm going to start a load of wash. When you come in, will you leave your clothes by the washer? Did you have any lunch? Do you want to take a shower first?"

David responded with, "Yes," "No," and "Yes."

Making her way into the kitchen, Chris walked past the wall phone and wondered when it would ring. *Just keep busy*, she told herself. *Otherwise you'll drive yourself crazy.*

She separated the dirty clothing and started a load of laundry, made a sandwich for David, and put a can of beer alongside his plate. After his shower she was certain he'd carry his lunch to the deck, where they ate most meals this time of year.

A few minutes later, the phone rang, and Chris immediately grabbed it, thinking it must be Ron. She was surprised to hear her brother Hal say, "Hey, Chris. What's up? I haven't heard from you in the past two days. Is everything all right?"

Chris, who was so faithful every day in calling her brother at the mill, realized she had been so caught up in her own cares and concerns that she wasn't thinking of anyone or anything outside of the immediate situation with Carl and Ron.

"Sorry, Hal. So much has been going on around here. I guess I've just gotten out of my normal routine. Is everything all right at the mill?"

She suddenly realized how totally overwhelmed she had been since Carl had first called her. She grabbed a sponge from the sink, rinsed it out, and wiped off the counters as she carried on her conversation with her brother.

"Everything's fine here. I promise to get back on track," Chris told her brother, knowing what a big lie that was. He didn't need to know what she and David were dealing with.

"Are you and David free to come out to the cottage anytime this week?" Hal asked. "Connie and I would love to spend some time with you. Give her a call and let her know—maybe Thursday or Friday for dinner? By the way, there's some good news you should know. Carol is engaged—not bad for our thirty-six-year-old daughter. She met Chad at the National Hardware Show in Vegas last year. He's from Binghamton. They're thinking of a Christmastime wedding. I'm sure Carol hasn't had a chance to call her godmother, but I know she won't mind my telling you."

"I'm so happy for her. I'll be sure to stop by the mill this week and see her. Maybe we can even do lunch," Chris said, thinking perhaps the activity might keep her mind occupied.

"That's a great idea, Chris. Maybe even you and I will have a chance to talk a bit," Hal said hopefully.

"I'll plan to do that. Oh, by the way, did I ever thank you for watering the hanging plants while we were at camp and keeping an eye on the place? I truly appreciate it."

David, who had just entered the kitchen and overheard the conversation, called out, "Thank you from me too, Hal."

Chris added, "I trust you heard that?"

"I did. Tell him he's very welcome. It was fun stopping by the place. All right, Chris. Call me tomorrow."

As Chris bid her good-byes, David announced that he was on his way to take a shower.

Chris put the phone back on the hook and walked back to the sink to replace the sponge. For the first time, she gave thought to how far she needed to go with the truth about Ron's father. Was there a need to tell Hal and Diane? And what about DeEtte?

She decided that if and when she next talked with Ron these were questions only he could answer.

Monday came and went. Tuesday came and passed—likewise, Wednesday, Thursday, Friday, and Saturday—without any word from Ron.

On Sunday Chris and David decided to walk the few blocks for the nine o'clock morning Mass at St. Mary's.

As they walked, David took Chris's hand and said, "It's been almost a week. What do you think Ron is doing?"

"My head has been filled with every wild thought imaginable. I think he's in his own world, needing to sort out how this news impacts the person he knows himself to be."

Depending on how Ron reacted to this recent revelation, she thought, *Will I share the details of his conception?* She mulled over just how she might share the story with Ron. Somewhere between the front steps of their home and the front steps of St. Mary's, she decided to answer any and all questions Ron might have. She, who had held on to so many secrets for so long, wanted to unburden herself, to be free of the bondage of harboring long-held secrets.

When the sun rose on Monday morning, Chris was sitting on the back deck sipping coffee and thoroughly enjoying the sounds of cardinals that sang from the top of the large ash at the side of the yard. An acrylic tube-style birdfeeder hung from a lower branch and had attracted not only the neighborhood squirrels but also a pair of mourning doves that gathered on the grass beneath it. Robins flitted about the dewy grass, as did chickadees and sparrows. She couldn't resist a smile, as she enjoyed this time, just at daybreak, when the natural world came alive. She waited for the first beams of sunrise to spread a spotlight on the tops of the trees.

She opened the morning paper that had been dropped on the front porch by the young man who conscientiously and consistently tossed it up on the welcome mat, rain or shine.

"Up a bit early, honey?" David's voice reached her through the screen. "Do you need a warm-up?"

"Yup!" Chris replied.

David walked out onto the deck, pushed up the umbrella that sat in the middle of the glass-topped round table, and sat down at an angle to Chris so he too had a full view of the backyard.

"Thanks. That looks a little better," Chris said.

David filled her coffee cup. "Any good news this morning?"

"I haven't really been paying much attention to the paper. Frankly the backyard activity is much more enjoyable."

"I'm getting a little concerned, Chris. I really thought we'd have heard from Ron by now."

"Me too. But I don't want to call him and force him into a premature decision. Even after my deceit, I don't want him to think that just because I'm his mother he has to do something because I'm asking. I want it to be his choice, his decision. He's the one who has to decide about being a bone marrow donor and have the procedure performed. It's one thing for me to think about what's good and right, but I'm not the one being poked and prodded. Ron has a lot to think about, not the least of which is the fact that he has a half-brother."

"I suppose you're right," David said. "But I know Ron, and I can't imagine his not responding to this situation without the utmost love and caring. Let's remember, that's who he is, the son we raised. Truly, Chris, the one thing that has gotten the better of me is the wait. What is that prayer you always say? 'Please God, give me patience, but be quick!' "

They both laughed as David's comment eased the tension, and they relaxed.

"OK, are you ready for some scrambled eggs and peppers?" Chris asked, as she headed for the sliding screen door.

"Sounds good."

They lingered over breakfast, and Chris finally settled back, reading the latest news. Shortly after seven the phone rang, and as Chris jumped up, she joyfully proclaimed, "Let's hope it's Ron."

She lifted the receiver and immediately headed back outside, so if it was Ron, David could share in the conversation. "Hello!" Chris answered.

"Good morning, Mom. I hope this isn't too early to call."

"Not at all, Ron," Chris said, trying to contain her excitement at finally hearing his voice. She moved alongside where David sat.

"Can I come by around nine thirty?" Ron asked. "I'll drive down right after seven-thirty Mass."

"We'll be here," his mother said.

"OK, Mom. See you then. I love you. Bye."

"That was short and sweet. I assume he's driving down to talk to us?" David asked, having picked up on Chris's comments.

"Yes, and he sounded fine. It was pleasant. He'll be here around nine thirty. Maybe I could make a quick kuchen, and while it's baking, I'll shower. Anything else you think I need to do before he arrives?"

"Will you relax and stop worrying if the bed is made and the kitchen floor is mopped? He's our son. This is our home, his home. Don't panic, Chris. It'll be all right. Didn't we both say he'd do the right thing? Let's just wait and see what he says," David said with a positive flair.

Chris couldn't help it; everything needed to be perfect in whatever way she could orchestrate this homecoming. When it came to her son, she would do whatever was necessary.

With an apricot-topped kuchen now in the oven, she ran up the stairs with the oven timer in hand. She quickly made the double bed then jumped into the shower. Toweling off, she glanced at the timer on her nightstand and noticed she still had twelve minutes before the kuchen was done. As she stood facing the mirror to blow-dry and style her hair, she noted that although her breasts sagged a bit and her skin wasn't as taut as in years past, she was grateful to still possess a body that reflected good health.

She pulled open a dresser drawer and chose a pair of tan Bermudas and a multicolored slip-on blouse. She walked down the stairs, passing David on his ascent as he announced it was his turn to take a shower. It would be another forty minutes before Ron arrived. She did a walkthrough of the main floor of the house, making sure everything was in its place, then returned to the deck to add a third placemat and napkin to the table.

The oven timer rang; she grabbed her oven mitts and removed the small cake from the oven. How many times had she made this German goody? Her mom had made this often, frequently after dinner for all to enjoy with a glass of milk before bedtime. Chris learned it had been her dad who had asked his mother to share the recipe with Mary Wright soon after their wedding. Hal, Sr., often told his children, "Your grandmother would get up early and make this so my brothers and I could have it for breakfast."

David appeared in the kitchen, looking and smelling so good, the odor of his aftershave momentarily replacing the aroma of the kuchen. Chris had first come to recognize the scent of David forty-five years earlier in their small office at the *Herald and Courier*. Some things didn't change, and she loved him for it; it was a reflection of the tradition and stability she valued.

"I'm going to make another pot of coffee and put some mugs and plates on the table," she reported to David.

He assisted Chris in making the table look as she wanted, then sat down with his laptop. Chris reopened the paper and, knowing she not only had the time but also needed to keep herself busy, started the sudoku on the funny page. "I can't believe I didn't bring a pen out here with me," she said, angry with herself, as she reentered the house to retrieve one.

After she returned to the deck, she was concentrating on the puzzle when she heard "Good morning," as Ron walked across the back lawn to the steps. Chris, not wanting to appear too enthusiastic, rose gently from her chair and gave Ron a hug; David did the same. "Another gorgeous morning to be out here," Ron exclaimed. David and Chris agreed.

"Coffee and kuchen?" Chris asked.

"I think I could smell this on my way down," Ron said. "Maybe it was wishful thinking."

Chris poured coffee from a thermal carafe then cut some squares of kuchen and placed a piece on everyone's plate.

As she sat down, Ron began, "I'm sure you've both been wondering what I've been thinking and been doing for the last week. First, Mom, here's your letter. I hope it's all right that I made a copy for myself."

Chris had noticed the letter in Ron's hand as he walked up the back steps and was grateful to receive it from him.

"I spent most of last Monday after you left sitting in church, trying to understand what transpired thirty-four years ago and the secret you two have kept all these years. I read and reread Mr. Taylor's letter. I only wish I had known him. I do remember when he spoke to me those nights in Cortland when I led that retreat, but as he said in the letter, he didn't introduce himself, and there was no reason for me to ask. I just thought he was one of the parishioners."

He paused and picked up the kuchen, took a bite, and chewed away. "It's always good when it's warm," he remarked. He drank some coffee to wash it down, then continued. "By the way, Mom, if you brought back the paper from camp with Fred's obituary, I'd like a copy to familiarize myself with his face. Anyway, by the late afternoon, I decided to call Father Jim at the Retired Priests' Center in Syracuse. I asked him if it was too late to take him out to dinner. He was pleased and asked if there was any special reason for our getting together. I simply said you had shared some news with me and I needed his advice. He said, 'I look forward to talking to you, Ron. It's long overdue.' "

David warmed up everyone's coffee; he was glad he'd left the pot on the table so he didn't have to miss a word.

Ron continued, "We had dinner at a great Italian restaurant in Little Italy on the north side of Syracuse. We've all got to go there for dinner real soon. The food was outstanding. Before we arrived, I e-mailed Father Jim a copy of the letter." He turned toward Chris. "I figured it would be all right, since you said he knew about the affair and your wish to keep the secret. He was so consoling, Mom, supporting you and Dad and your desire over the years to maintain that I was your son. But he did add that when I entered the priesthood he did lean on you to share the truth with me. He said he thought I could have handled it and been able to deal with the issue discreetly." Ron paused momentarily to catch his breath.

Chris took note that he was speaking pleasantly, but it wasn't his usual tone of voice; rather it was a bit standoffish and more businesslike.

"By the end of dinner," Ron went on, "Father Jim was so happy, and honestly, Mom, as much as was on my mind, he talked about you, that the secret was now out in the open, and that you didn't need to hide this anymore. Over some cannoli he asked me what I was going to do about Carl's request. I told him I hadn't figured that out yet—not that I wouldn't help out, but just at this point, I didn't know exactly how to handle it. When I dropped him off, he asked that you call him, Mom. He said you haven't driven to Syracuse for three months for spiritual direction, and he misses you."

Chris smiled at the thought of Father Jim saying that. How old was he now? Eighty-five? She was happy he was living out his retirement with active priestly responsibilities at the assisted-living center that was run by the diocese. He still impressed her with his mental faculties, which were sharp as ever. Whenever they met, he regularly shared the latest books he'd read, both religious and secular, and over the years had recommended many of the tomes that now lined her bookshelves. She thought of the countless hours over the past thirty-plus years that she had spent with him and wondered how she would have survived without his guidance. She now assured Ron, "I'll call and schedule a visit this week."

"On Tuesday, after I said morning Mass," Ron continued, "I called information and asked for Carl Taylor's number."

Only now did Chris realize that in the heat of their conversation she never had given Ron the sheet of paper Carl had handed her with his contact information.

"Carl answered the phone and was very pleasant," Ron said. "He was pleased that I had called so soon after your meeting with him. We talked for almost an hour, both of us coming to the realization that although he's old enough to be my father, we're half-brothers. He asked if I'd be willing to meet him the next day at his doctor's office at University Upstate Hospital."

"Oh, my gosh! You've already seen Carl?" Chris said, surprised.

"Last Wednesday in Syracuse," Ron confirmed. "What a great doctor he has handling his case. Although Carl has lost weight and has had some side effects from medications, the doctor said he's in good physical condition, which should bode well for his recovery, if there's a match. We talked, and the doctor arranged for me to be tested while I was there. We won't know for a few days whether I'm a match. The doctor explained the entire procedure—the operation that will take place if they can use my bone marrow. He said if I'm compatible he might be able to schedule the transplant in the next week or two. He's got my cell number, so I should hear from him anytime now. Isn't modern medicine awesome?" Ron said, glancing at his parents for agreement and receiving it.

"After we finished up with the doctor," he went on, "Carl asked if I had time to go to the cafeteria with him for coffee. He had a small briefcase with him and took out a scrapbook and a photo album. I couldn't believe it—he had pictures of you and Grandma and Grandpa, Uncle Hal, and Aunt Diane in front of the camp in 1957. He showed me a scrapbook of his dad and some of the articles about him and his band. He also had pictures of his family. Carl is a good man."

There was now silence around the table; everyone continued to drink and eat, not saying a word.

"Can I ask what made you decide to help Carl?" Chris finally asked Ron.

"I asked myself the same question," Ron said. "If it were anyone and anyplace else and I was a match, wouldn't I, in good conscience, give my bone marrow? The process is simple, and it shouldn't have any long-term effects for me. But hopefully it'll give Carl his life back. How could I deny him that? Even without my being a priest, I believe—I know—it's the right thing to do. And I'm comfortable with my decision."

"Thank you for doing this," Chris said. "I know you've had to deal with an awful lot of emotional information this last week, and again I want you to know how sorry I am. I hope in time you can forgive me for all these years of deceit."

"Mom, I've thought long and hard about it. But one thing that Mr. Taylor said in his letter really stayed with me—that he was grateful that you never contacted him, as he thought it would have ruined his marriage and devastated Carl. I did ask Carl how he felt when he received his letter, after not knowing the truth all these years. He said that since, at this point in time, he couldn't change anything, he wasn't going to worry or be concerned about what might have been. But he did say, as crazy as it sounds, 'Thank God for your mother bringing you into the world, because you might be my only hope for survival.' So here we are." There was a pause, and then Ron turned to his father. "You know, Dad, you've been very quiet through all this. What are your feelings?"

David had been focusing intently on Ron as he spoke. He drew in a breath and, through a wave of emotion, said, "You'll always be my son, Ron. I couldn't be happier to call you my own. Perhaps you have different feelings right now after learning about Fred Taylor, but as far as I'm concerned, nothing has changed."

"Thanks, Dad. I couldn't have said it any better. That's how I feel. I'm *your* son and always will be. I couldn't have asked for a better father to raise me." Ron reached out and grabbed his father's hand. "I tried to relive all our conversations over the years as I thought about us this past week. I'm pretty sure the fact that I wasn't your biological son impacted you when Greg was killed."

Ron was cognizant of his father's sensitivity. They had spoken of Greg regularly in the past, and David's eyes became glassy whenever Greg's name was mentioned, even now after nineteen years.

"I reflected on our relationship over the years, Dad. I remember after Greg was killed how confrontational you became. I thought it was just that you missed him and were taking it out on me somehow. I knew I could never measure up to him, but I had no idea at the time that he was your only biological son. I hope I have a better understanding today of your emotions back then. I'm just glad that our strained relationship only lasted a couple of years, and then you seemed to get back to normal." Ron let go of his dad's hand. "Greg's death was a big loss for me too. He was ten years older than me, so he always was my big brother.

Chris nodded in agreement, unsure if she had ever heard Ron share his feelings about Greg quite like this. "I always looked up to him—how strong he was, how well he played sports, how good-looking he was, how well he always dressed." David was listening intently and wiped a tear from his cheek. "Even before he became a marine, don't you think he mentally was one of them? He took such good care of me and was always willing to play, even though we didn't have much in common. His death was such a loss for all of us."

"The most important thing I've decided," Ron said, "is that we can all keep the secret. The fact that I now know the truth is what's important, although I have to confess, as easy as it is for me to forgive you both, it's still very hard on me emotionally to try to internalize the whole thing. That's going to take some time. I don't think anyone else will benefit from knowing that Carl and I are half-brothers. If there's ever a time when our family and Carl are together, couldn't we say Carl reached out to apologize for his dad's hurtful decision of not allowing contact between the two of you? I don't think we'd be lying; we simply wouldn't complicate people's lives with more information than they really need. What do you think?"

"Honestly, Ron," Chris said, "I hadn't even thought that far. But that would certainly work for me. What about you, David?"

With apparently much forethought, David responded, "Well, it seems to me that if none of Carl's daughters were matches, they're certainly going to want to know who the donor is. I'm not sure how you'll work around that, Ron. Who knows, though? Maybe there's a way. And let's remember, we're talking about a lot of 'ifs' and 'buts,' when we don't even know if Ron is a match. There's no guarantee just because he's Carl's half-brother."

Chris breathed a sigh of relief. Her son had come home.

CHAPTER 18

David placed the canoe on a carrier and wheeled it from the side of the camp, where it had been resting on a pair of well-worn sawhorses. Since the middle of May, each week he and Chris had made the trek to camp, discovering that in retirement one didn't have to wait until the weekend to "go to camp." Chris continued her thorough spring housecleaning there, and David took on a labor of love. For Chris's birthday, he had promised to strip the old cedar canoe of its varnish and redo it for her.

"When we put it back in the water, do we get to christen it with a bottle of Champagne?" Chris asked.

"I think we'd best just drink the bubbly and forget about bottles breaking on wooden bows," David smartly replied.

He had spent hours in work clothes, even using a facemask as he removed old varnish, sanded, spread linseed oil inside and out, and finally shellacked and varnished the boat his father-in-law had built at the mill sixty years before. David had known that when Hal, Sr., was still alive, every few years he paid someone to do the dirty job David had spent the last month performing.

David had taken on the job as a challenge to himself; he never had done anything like this before. Halfway through the project, he gave serious question to his sanity. As labor-intensive as the endeavor had been, when he had completed it last weekend, he had covered the canoe with the tarp, after taking some pictures to compare to the ones he had taken before he had started the project.

Chris now looked at her father's pride and joy as it sat on a wide swath of grass by the dock. It was a work of art, and with its new coat of varnish, it sparkled in the early-June sunlight.

"David, you must be so proud of yourself. It's gorgeous," Chris commented, as she wrapped her arms around him. "Thank you so much. I couldn't have received a better present. It looks like a brand-new canoe. My dad would be so happy. After I finish up cleaning, I'll take it out on its maiden voyage. It is seaworthy, right?"

"After all the coats I put on, it had better be," David said with a laugh. "Take along a bailing can just in case you spot a leak."

Chris heard the phone ring. "I'll get it," she said.

The temperature was creeping into the eighties as Chris heard the screen door slam behind her. She picked up the phone on the forth ring.

"Mom, it looks like I'll be able to get to camp tomorrow by noon. I've asked Father Tom, the Newman Chaplin at the college, if he'd mind saying the eleven o'clock Mass. He said yes, so I'll scoot after the nine o'clock service," Ron reported.

Replacing the receiver, Chris thought about all the years when there had been no phone at camp; she wondered how they had survived. How strange it was. When she first came to experience camp, there was no electricity, no inside plumbing except for the water pump, and no phone. Somehow those days were far simpler, less complex than today's camp. She had grown used to the conveniences, however, and wasn't about to give them up.

She was grateful that it felt more like home now, with well-appointed rooms and all the amenities one could want. And then there was the unchanging scenery: the Adirondacks, the mountains, the lakes, and the hiking trails. She was so grateful to every man and woman who had served on the committees, clubs, and agencies that had fought to keep the park forever wild. Just as she'd been able to derive so much pleasure from this region, she hoped not only that her children's children would enjoy this special part of New York State but also that it would remain as it was for count-less generations to come.

"David, Ron says he'll be here by noon tomorrow," Chris called out from the front porch.

"That's great," David yelled back.

He was sliding the canoe into the water alongside the dock. He already had flipped the aluminum rowboat and tied it to the oppo-site side of the dock, as along with the recently acquired kayak. Ron had found kayaking was much more to his liking, although he continued to use the canoe occasionally.

Chris returned to her cleaning; guests were coming, and she wanted everything to be perfect before tomorrow.

When Sunday morning arrived, Chris wondered whether the Taylors or Ron would arrive first, or if they might even arrive simul-taneously. *Carl said he and his wife Susan would be getting on the road at nine, so they'll probably be here by twelve,* she thought. *Ron usually runs a little late; he's like me—if you're there before it's over, you're there on time.*

When Chris had called Carl three weeks earlier to suggest a possible joint weekend at camp, he had thanked her and won-dered if a Sunday-Monday stay - over would work for them. Carl was back volunteering for youth sport activities in the community and was so enjoying his new lease on life that he didn't want to forego a Saturday working with the kids.

"Isn't that the beauty of retirement, Carl?" Chris had asked him. She said that a Sunday arrival would work perfectly. During the rather lengthy phone conversation, she had asked if he would bring along his pictures he had shared with Ron nine months earlier.

Reflecting on that chat, she walked over to the camp book-shelves to retrieve her mom's photo albums, which she was certain Carl would get a kick out of. She lugged the three albums, two of which had nothing to do with Carl but showed the camp's interior improvements over the years. Perhaps Carl might like to see how the place had evolved. She laid them out on the dining room table.

Oh, God, she thought. *What have I gotten myself into?*

She walked to the fireplace and rested her hands on the stone mantle as she stared at the wood-framed photo of her parents that stood front and center.

"Mom and Dad, you've got to help me out," she said. "Please let this day go well."

She knew how grateful Carl and Susan were for Carl's recovery, but she had no idea what Susan's thinking was when it came to Chris's past relationships with both Carl and his father. She just hoped, now that Susan knew the history, that any conversations between them would be comfortable and nonjudgmental. She had spoken with Susan countless times on the phone since last August, but they hadn't yet met face to face, and Chris wouldn't have been able to pick her out in a crowd.

Let's just hope for the best, she prayed.

Chris wasn't sure what motivated her to re-climb the staircase to the loft, but she seemed drawn to the second floor. She had spent several hours yesterday making sure the rooms were clean, the curtains washed, and the furniture dusted.

For the overnight she'd invite Carl and Susan to occupy what had been her parents' bedroom on the main floor, where they would have easy access to the bathroom, and leave Ron to sleep upstairs, if he decided to stay over. She had no doubt there would be a tour of the camp, and as usual, she wanted everything to be just right.

Walking through the first bedroom and into the adjoining space, she smiled, as the room seemed to glow. The pine plank flooring and cedar walls continued to look as radiant as always. The brass bed sat against the large loft window at the end of the room. Sunlight poured through the four-pane window and the calico drapes her mother had fashioned twenty-five years ago. She sat down at the foot of the bed and embraced the bedpost.

So much has transpired in our lives over the past nine months, Chris thought. *Have any of us really taken the time to fully absorb the impact, the emotional toll it's taken on our lives?*

Her vision was as clear as if it had happened the day before—the memory of Ron's phone call that Monday after he had met with them on the back deck.

"Mom, Carl's doctor just called. I'm a match," Ron had reported.

As overjoyed as she had been at the news, Chris recalled the disappointment when Ron told her, quite emphatically, that he would feel much better if she and his father stayed put in Cooperstown and let him and Carl deal with this on their own. He was confident he could handle the procedure, and there was no need for concern or worry.

At the time all Chris could think of was twenty years earlier when Ron, at age twelve, had been hit by a car as he rode his bicycle home from baseball practice. She and David had kept vigil at the hospital, praying for his recovery. There were no broken bones but lots of bangs and bruises; the most serious injury was that he had hit his head and had been knocked unconscious.

They were so grateful to the hospital staff and their answered prayers when Ron recovered within a week and returned home. Chris often wondered whether the concussion Ron suffered might have been a turning point in his young life. His doctor had shared with them that it was critical that Ron avoid any activity in which he might receive another blow to the head. Reluctantly Ron stopped playing contact team sports, where the potential of injury was high, and engaged in recreational swimming and jogging on his own.

Unsure whether Ron worried that the concussion might have long-term effects on his mental faculties, Chris and David noticed how he worked at becoming a better student; he improved his grades over the next few years and earned an invitation to the National Honor Society. At the dinner table, when the meal was finished and the family regularly engaged in discussions of current events, it became apparent that Ron was developing a growing interest in reading and history. He became more disciplined when it came to his piano lessons and even kept a little record book of the time he spent practicing each day.

Twenty years ago Ron had read everything available about concussions and their long-term effects. Chris had no doubt he had likewise searched the Internet for information on bone marrow transplants and how they impacted the donor.

"Mom, did you know that a man named Dr. E. Donnall Thomas did research regarding bone marrow at Mary Bassett Hospital in Cooperstown? He received the Nobel Prize in Medicine in nineteen ninety for developing a process for bone marrow transplantation as a treatment for leukemia patients," Ron had told Chris over the phone. "He would have been on staff there when you were in high school," he added. "At least that's what I read on the Internet." Ron was, in fact, doing his homework.

After undergoing the bone marrow transplant withdrawal procedure, Ron contacted Chris. "The doctors told me I'll be a little tired and maybe a bit stiff over the next few weeks," he said, "but they gave me an anesthetic, and I felt nothing during the procedure. I hope the same is true for Carl. He told me he'd be in isolation for a week, and he'll probably need a blood transfusion or two and some antibiotics. Keep praying, Mom."

Chris remembered how relieved she was that Ron had made it through the procedure and hoped she could feel the same soon when she heard from Carl.

Susan, Carl's wife, had called that same evening. David had answered the phone, and she had assured him and Chris that everything had gone successfully. She said Carl would be isolated and basically shared the same information Ron had in his call.

"Carl's being restricted and can't call you himself, but I'm sure he'll contact you when he's free and clear," Susan added. "Thanks again for everything. We so appreciate your help. I just got off the phone with Ron and expressed our thanks. It sounds to me that he came through with flying colors. I'm so happy to hear that."

Chris had been lighting candles at St. Mary's and saying novenas, even praying for the intercession of blessed Kateri Tekakwitha for Carl's full and complete recovery, remembering as a child her mother's reference to this Native American Indian as the "Lily of the Mohawk." Chris had asked everyone she knew to pray for him, simply telling them that a friend of theirs was being treated for cancer.

The phone call from Carl ten days later was one of the best Chris could remember in recent years.

"All went well," Carl had said. "Thank you again. The doctor is sending me home. He's pleased with the transplant and the success of the antiviral drugs and tells me I'll need to take it easy for the next six weeks. We should have an idea then how successful this procedure has been. Keep the prayers coming, Chris. I think they're helping."

As they said their good-byes, Carl indicated that in six weeks, when he had his appointment with his doctor, he'd give her a call and update her on his progress. She told him to remain positive, as she was confident of good news.

"Stay well, Carl. Relax and recover. Talk to you soon. Take care." As she replaced the receiver that warm September afternoon, Chris had uttered, "Thank you, dear God." and David added, "I'll say that again. Thank you, God."

The next six weeks seemed to float by, with Ron's health back to normal. She was overjoyed with his smooth and rapid recovery, but she was concerned that their mother-son communications hadn't returned to their pre-August days. With the recent trauma now passed, Chris wondered whether Ron was still having mixed feelings about his commitment to the priesthood. She didn't ask, and he didn't mention it.

Six weeks later Carl called with the best news ever. His cancer was in remission, and the doctor was optimistic that in six months he'd be cleared. "The doctor told me, 'Go live your life,' " Carl told her. " 'Enjoy every minute. You've earned it.' "

"Your voice sounds so strong. Did the doctor say you were good for ten years or fifty thousand miles, whichever comes first?" Chris asked, laughing.

"It was something like that. What a new lease on life I have. I know I've said this over and over, but thank you. What a gift I've been given. Life!"

Ron would tell his mother that when Carl had phoned him he had begun with, "Thanks, brother. I received some very good news today, thanks to you. There will never be enough words to thank you, Ron, for your gift of life to me. I'll always be indebted."

Chris looked about the loft, grateful for this time of solitude and reflection. She glanced down at Grandma Wright's patchwork quilt, which once again seemed to be providing her comfort and warmth, stability and grounding. She thought of the many members of her extended family—disorganized, miles apart, following the beat of their own drummers—and yet when these "people pieces" were sewn together, somehow miraculously the family came together as a cohesive, beautiful unit.

It had been the words of Father Jim re-enforcing her strong family values and love that had moved her to a place of peace the last September. Remembering Ron's words that Father Jim had missed seeing her, she had called and set an appointment. While Ron was helping Carl, she could help her own spiritual growth.

Their one-hour session took place on a park bench on the side lawn of his living center. Amid the splendid colors of a Central New York autumn, they talked. Without apology or dramatics, Chris finally was able to look her spiritual director of thirty-five-plus years and share with him the many things she had kept to herself for so long.

"You know, Father Jim, I didn't want to think of myself as a bad girl. I didn't want to disappoint my parents. I felt I had to be perfect.

I came home from that time at camp feeling so sinful, so unclean, so damaged. I created a story I could live with. I was so ashamed."

"Welcome to the real world," Father Jim had told her. "Isn't it interesting to admit you are human, that you have faults and failings and are far from perfect? The most important thing is that you've always known that God loves you and has forgiven you a hundred times over, even if you couldn't forgive yourself. I certainly hope you can now. I know it's going to take some time for Ron to put all this information into perspective, but you have to know that not for a minute has he not loved you and David as the caring parents he has always known."

His words reassured Chris tremendously. When their time together came to an end, she felt at peace. She was finally free.

The patchwork quilt seemed to put the last nine months into perspective, the things that survive through good times and bad, providing families, especially her own, a splendid symmetry... continuity.

David's voice jolted her back to reality. "Chris, are you in here?"

"I'm up here. I'll be right down," she called out, as she rose from her seat on the quilt, straightened it, and proceeded down the stairs.

"I hear someone coming down the driveway," David told her.

Chris found him waiting for her in the center of the living room, and she approached him and gave him a hug. "I've been thinking about everything that has happened since last August. How true it is that in hindsight we have twenty-twenty vision. I wonder why I ever was concerned, worried so much about how all of this would play out. Could we have asked for anything more?" Chris asked, as she looked into David's eyes. He gave her another hug and suggested they'd best check to see who had arrived.

The Ford Taurus came to rest alongside the Chrysler, and as Carl and Susan emerged, David and Chris were right there beside them, exchanging greetings and hugs.

"It looks a little familiar, Chris, but I'm expecting a full tour of the camp and grounds sometime during our stay," Carl requested.

"It's on the agenda. Please come on in," Chris offered, as she helped Susan gather a few things from the car.

Carl popped the trunk, and the men managed to pull out the luggage and other assorted briefcases and boxes.

"We're going to put you two in the back bedroom," Chris announced. "It's the room my mom and dad always used, and we still refer to it as their room."

Momentarily Carl stopped in his tracks, set down the luggage, and spread out his arms. Taking a deep breath, he said, "Yes! Oh, this smells so good. This I vividly remember. It looks to be a great few days weather-wise. I hope we can spend a lot of time outside."

David responded, "That we will do, Carl."

They entered the camp as David led the way. He and Carl deposited their belongings in the room they would occupy for their stay. Susan followed Chris and reported that in her basket and shopping bag she had brought along some food items they might enjoy. She opened the picnic basket and brought out a casserole of baked beans and a fresh loaf of bread. Then from the canvas bag came three bottles of wine from the Finger Lakes region of the state.

"I guess we're going to do some serious celebrating over the next couple of days," Chris noted.

David and Carl had joined the women in the kitchen. David, spying the bottles of wine, announced, "My kind of people. What can we get you? Coffee? Beer? Wine? A soft drink? I always say that if I haven't stocked it, you probably don't need it."

Carl announced he'd love a beer, as did Susan. David and Chris decided to join them. They were all still laughing from David's comment as he pulled the cans of beer from the refrigerator, when a loud "Hello" was heard as Ron walked in.

Seeing them all together, he broke out into a broad smile; in fact he beamed! He unceremoniously dropped his small duffel bag in the hall and, without breaking his stride, headed into the kitchen. Immediately Ron walked into the open arms of Carl, who embraced him in what could only be described as a bear hug. They lingered, then parted slightly, holding onto each other by the forearms; tears filled their eyes.

Susan broke the tension with, "OK, you two. You'd better stop that before you have all of us crying."

And she was right; moist eyes were apparent among the five of them. Chris, conscious of the tears, grabbed a box of tissues from the counter and passed them around. For the next minute, the only sound in the kitchen, besides the opening of beer cans, was people blowing their noses.

Ron said, "Boy, Carl, it's good to see you. How much weight have you gained?" Chris hadn't thought to mention that upon his arrival, but it was very apparent that his health and appetite had improved over the last few months.

"Would you like to sit on the porch or out on the dock?" Chris asked.

"Maybe the dock for a little while," Carl responded, "but let me grab my hat and sunscreen."

They moved out onto the porch. A few moments later, Carl joined them, his baseball cap now on his head and sunscreen in hand. They all proceeded slowly to the dock.

"Wow, this is just as I remember it," Carl said.

Ron was carrying two folding lawn chairs from the porch to add to the three at the end of the dock. By the time everyone arrived, he had arranged them in a tight semicircle.

"I can't believe it's been fifty-four years since I last sat on this dock," Carl said.

"Well, it's a dock," Chris said, "but it's no longer the original one. The old wooden one was replaced a couple of times over the years. Winters in the Adirondacks can have their way with a wooden dock. This metal one, with this nice covering, was installed five years ago. Hopefully it will outlast us."

"When did your mother and father die?" Carl asked her.

For the next hour, Chris discussed the passing of her parents, the improvements to the camp over the years, and her and David's family. Susan shared memories of the Taylor family and the passing of her mother-in-law, Helen.

The black flies were becoming a bit pesky, the large citronella candle on the dock doing little to deter them. David suggested that he barbecue some hot dogs and that they eat lunch indoors.

Over cooked wieners, baked beans, and potato salad, talk of their families continued. Chris poured cups of coffee and placed a bowl of fresh sliced fruit and five berry bowls on the table. As they passed the compote and helped themselves, Carl shared some new information.

"Because my dad died when I was in treatment, we never did anything to his house until this spring. He left the house to me, and I guess he assumed at some point we would sell it. Over the past couple of years before he died, he had suggested to my girls that one of them buy it, but they weren't interested, so he stayed in the place until his death. He had some help near the end of his life, but he managed quite well for his ninety years."

He took a pause, taking a spoonful of fruit and a sip of black coffee, then continued, "We had a couple of clean-out days. Our son-in-laws really helped out, as did the grandkids. I took the responsibility for my father's personal things—the desk, dresser, and closet." Carl stopped abruptly. Standing up from his chair, he said, "Let me go get something for you, Chris."

Moments later he returned from the bedroom, where his bags and boxes had been placed. He sat back down in his seat and placed a small white box, tied with a string, on the table. It was half the size of a shirt box but just as deep; Chris saw some writing on the top.

"When I cleaned out my dad's desk, I found this box in one of the drawers." Handing it to Chris, he said, "As you can see, Chris, it says to give it to you."

Chris read the words that were printed in black magic marker, PLEASE GIVE THIS BOX TO CHRISTINE WRIGHT HERRING. Below, in smaller writing, he had written her address.

Carl continued, "I knew we'd be getting together soon after I found this in March. I hope I haven't waited too long to get it to you, Chris. Please don't feel you have to open it here. I know it could be very personal."

Chris held the box in her hand, detecting that everyone around the table had their eyes glued on it. All she could think of was the line sung by Julie Andrews in *The Sound of Music,* "Brown paper packages tied up with string. These are a few of my favorite things…"

"I've held on to so many secrets for so many years," Chris said, "that I can't imagine anything is in this box that I won't be able to share with all of you."

She discovered the string was tied much too tightly for her to undo. David, sitting next to her, reached into his pants pocket and withdrew his handy jackknife. After he pulled out the blade and sliced through the string, Chris carefully took the lid off the box. On top was a white business-size envelope addressed to "The Reverend Ronald Herring."

"Well, Ron, this is for you," Chris said, as she handed it to him at the end of the table. Beneath the envelope she saw a CD, which she removed from the box. It appeared to be a self-recorded disc, as there was no seal around it or commercial picture or writing. There was a handwritten note beneath it. Chris removed it and read it aloud.

Dear Chris,

I remember how much you enjoyed listening to Dave Brubeck back in 1976. My group, The Blue Notes, made a recording around 1980 of some of the numbers we were playing at the time, including "Take Five." I also included a few other numbers that might be meaningful. A few years ago, I had a friend transfer the tape to a CD. I hope you enjoy it and remember me.

Fred

"You know, the week I met your father he had his saxophone with him and told me he planned to practice and work on a few new arrangements for the group. What a nice memory." Chris was doing her best to keep her emotions under control and not share any more than was necessary about her memories of that fateful evening.

Ron was still holding the envelope in his hand, letting his mother take the floor. Finally he picked up his butter knife, wiped it on his paper napkin, and slit the envelope open. As he opened the letter, he grabbed a check that had slipped out and looked at it. "Oh, my God," he said. He placed the check behind the letter and read the note out loud.

Dear Son,

In so many ways, Ron, calling you "son" after all these years seems a little strange for me. I just wanted you to know, before I died, how much you were thought of and loved, from afar, albeit in silence.

Because I did nothing for you during my lifetime, I thought in some way I could make up for that in death. I know you're very involved with youth programs and refugee resettlement at your church and in your community. Nothing would make me happier than to have you use the enclosed check to carry on the work you feel so passionate about. I'm doing this for you now, as I didn't include you in my will for obvious reasons.

Carl and his family have been taken care of, so please don't feel as if they were overlooked in any way because of this gift to you. I leave it up to you to decide if you'd like to share this note with Carl.

I will be eternally grateful to your mother for carrying the burden of secrecy all these years and, more important, to your father, David, for apparently raising you as his own.

As you never tried to make contact with me, I assume you didn't know about my being your father until after my death.

I'm sure by now your mother has shared with you the letter she should have received after my death, wherein I shared that I met you in 2009 in Cortland. I didn't want to betray your mother and father's secret, but having the chance to shake your hand and talk to you was one of the highlights of my life. I hope that you live a long, full, and happy life.

Love,
Your father

Tears welled up in Ron's eyes. He paused momentarily then spoke. "Isn't it strange?" Turning to Carl, somehow forgetting that they shared a father, he said, "Could your dad ever have imagined that we'd all be sitting around this table as I read this letter?" He looked at the check again and said to Carl, "I hope your father was a wealthy man, because this check is for a hundred thousand dollars." There were audible gasps around the table.

Carl spoke first. "He wasn't wealthy, but he did accumulate savings throughout his lifetime and had some very successful investments that survived the drop in the market over the past few years. We sold his house for a good price in May, so he was right in saying we were well taken care of. I think he also may have had an idea that you'd be there for me in my need, and how else could he say, 'Thank you'?"

"Wow! I'm speechless. I couldn't have imagined anything like this and frankly never gave it a thought. I'm truly overwhelmed," Ron confessed.

Chris sat in deep thought, contemplating thirty-four years of keeping her secret. She now felt validated that she had made the right choice, as difficult as it had been on her conscience.

She rose from the table, CD in hand, and walked to the kitchen counter, where a radio/CD player sat. After she inserted the CD and pushed "play," she heard the beginning notes. It wasn't what she had expected. She took her place at the dining room table with the others. She recognized the Beatles classic, "Let It Be."

EPILOGUE

It was August 2011, one year since Chris's world had come crashing down around her. She looked back on all the events that had unfolded and was grateful they'd had such a positive outcome. Water poured off the camp roof as she stood arm in arm with David, enjoying the sound of the rain as it pelted the metal roof above. The Sunday afternoon was hot, and the rain was a welcome relief, bringing not only the temperature down but also the humidity.

It had been a glorious summer at Lake Wrights. Commemorating ten years since their father had died, Diane and Hal, Jr., had brought their families to camp. Even DeEtte had journeyed north from Atlanta to join the family reunion. Although the year had been tumultuous for Chris, no one in the family was any wiser to the events that she David, and Ron had experienced.

Six weeks after Ron had received his surprise check from Fred Taylor, he had invited his mom and dad to dinner in Utica. En route, Chris and David wondered whether, after a year of discernment, Ron finally had arrived at a decision about his vocation. Was he about to share good news with them?

To their delight and surprise, there was a decision but one they hadn't foreseen. When they arrived to pick Ron up at the rectory, he asked that they exit the car and walk across the street with him to a three-story brick storefront under renovation.

"I wanted you two to know that after I donated Fred's check to the church," Ron told them, "the parish council and I decided to purchase this building for a hospitality center to be used with our refugees and youth. Wait until you see the work our parishioners have done. I can't believe the donations of materials we've received from the community. So many people—not only folks from St. Anne's but also from other churches—have called or stopped by to see what they could do to help. Once news got out that all were welcome here, enthusiasm for the project grew and grew. What a great experience this has been."

Chris and David stood in the center of a large gathering area.

"Does this mean you'll be staying on at St. Anne's for a bit to oversee the center's completion and startup?" David asked.

"You bet!" Ron told them. "I guess your real question, Dad, is whether I've decided to stay with the priesthood. You know, Fred's check really enabled me to think outside my own concerns and focus on projects I've been passionate about for so long. His gift to me has been the leavening for this center. We've already raised an equal amount through in-kind services and community support." He continued as he led his parents on a tour. "Our target opening date is September tenth. I sure hope you both can be here for the ribbon cutting. I've even called Carl and asked him if he'd like to see how his dad's money is being used."

As the rain eased up, David turned to Chris. "Honey, is it possible we survived all that we have faced? And I must tell you, given the situation we were facing last year, could either of us have imagined how well everything would work out?"

"You've got that right," Chris said. "In many ways things kept unfolding for us—first Ron's decision to help Carl, and then Carl's recovery, and then Ron's willingness to forgive us after we kept him in the dark for so many years."

The storm was moving on, but occasional lightning strikes still flashed as thunder echoed off the mountains. David took Chris by the hand and led her toward the dock. She noticed a few of the hardwoods across the lake were already tinged with orange. *It's that time of the year,* she thought. *Another season at camp draws to a close.*

They stood staring out at a very calm lake. There was no breeze; everything was still.

"I never did ask about your spiritual-direction session the other day with Father Jim," David said. "You just told me he said to say hi and that he looked fine. Did he have any comments about Carl's phone call, or is that too confidential for you to share with me?"

"No, nothing I can't share. He was just surprised that Carl had waited so long to tell me the truth about his father. But then he said, 'Maybe he needed time to think about it.' "

A few weeks after Carl and Susan had come to camp, Carl called one morning and asked if Chris had a few minutes while he shared some background about his father. She had been a bit surprised. At camp she and Carl had spent some time alone, with the opportunity for him to talk about his father. But Chris hadn't raised his father's name after that first meal at camp, and neither had he.

Carl had begun, "Chris, I know we didn't talk about my dad much at your camp, but I wanted to call and set the record straight. I got to thinking about some of the things you shared with me at the diner, almost a year ago now, and I need to set the record straight."

Chris had no idea where this conversation was headed.

Carl continued, "My dad was a philanderer. Once he formed his combo and was out on the road playing events, he started playing around. It was about the time when I got married that people started dropping hints. I never questioned my father and always worried about my mother finding out. It wasn't until she was near death that she told me she had known that my dad had been a womanizer. She said she wanted me to know because she always prayed that I wouldn't follow his example."

Chris envisioned tears welling up in Carl's eyes as he mentioned his mother.

"My mom was such a great lady, and she loved my dad and me. She adored Susan and my girls. You can imagine her not wanting them to be exposed to anything like this." Carl took a breather; Chris said nothing.

"Before any more time passed, Chris, I felt you should know so you didn't think this was your fault. I'm sure the first time my dad saw you that rainy morning, he was already hatching his plan to seduce you. That's who he had become. I just wanted to say that this wasn't your fault, and I hope that after all these years you can forgive him."

Hearing Carl's last statement, Chris said, "I appreciate what you're telling me, Carl. You also need to know that I forgave your father long ago. It'll be thirty-five years next month since I last saw your father. I've put the memory to rest."

Chris now slipped her arm around David. "Father Jim thought it was important for me to know the motivations behind Fred's actions. He said it might lighten the burden I've carried all these years."

"Well, has it?" David asked.

"I don't know if it makes any difference," Chris responded. "Now that I've been able to speak the truth to Ron, I'm at peace. I sense that he is too. It'll always be a part of me; it's who I am. But I can live with it. As long as I have you in my life, David, I can deal with anything. If I've learned one thing in thirty-five years of marriage, that's it."

The sun peeked out from behind the clouds. Blue skies were returning to Lake Wrights.

CPSIA information can be obtained at www.ICGtesting.com
Printed in the USA
LVOW06s1630171113

361643LV00017B/1262/P